It Takes a Thief

LOVESWEPT®
Kay Hooper
It Takes a Thief

Doubleday

NEW YORK • LONDON • TORONTO • SYDNEY • AUCKLAND

All of the characters in this book
are fictitious, and any resemblance
to actual persons, living or dead,
is purely coincidental

LOVESWEPT®
Published simultaneously in hardcover by Doubleday
and in paperback by Bantam, which are divisions of
Bantam Doubleday Dell Publishing Group, Inc.,
666 Fifth Avenue, New York, New York 10103

LOVESWEPT, DOUBLEDAY, and the portrayal of the wave device
are registered trademarks of
Bantam Doubleday Dell Publishing Group, Inc.

Library of Congress Cataloging-in-Publication Data
Hooper, Kay.
    It takes a thief / by Kay Hooper.—1st hardcover ed.
        p.   cm.
    ISBN 0-385-26075-X
    I. Title.
PS3558.058718   1989
813'.54—dc19   88-8526
                                                CIP

OG

It Takes a Thief

Prologue

He was a rotund little man, an unashamed paunch straining the seams of his tailored vest. Shiny wing-tipped shoes were on his small feet. He had a great leonine head with a cherub's face, small brightly twinkling eyes, and pouty lips. He was very much a caricature of a strutting bantam rooster pleased with his own importance; few of the people he casually encountered would see more than a vain little man.

There were those who knew better. A small number, certainly. They had learned their lesson, and knew that the man who called himself Hagen was as harmless as a battleship, as innocent as a shark in bloody waters, as foolish and inconsequential as an atomic bomb. They knew, in fact, that he possessed a Machiavellian mind of frightening ruthlessness, an absolute vision of justice, and an inability to give up even when the cause seemed lost.

And he was a rotten loser.

On this clear summer afternoon he was harshly reprimanding one of his newest men. "You were unforgivably clumsy. You set off an alarm that roused the entire building. Your orders were to verify that Josh Long had not returned to his apartment—and that was all! You were *not* told to attempt entry of the apartment."

Brady Seton had been a marine; he had grown up in one of the roughest sections of Chicago; and no one had ever called him a timid man. But now, standing stiffly before his boss's desk, he felt decidedly shaky. He had loused up badly, and he knew it; his first, relatively simple, assignment as an operative in the agency Hagen ran looked as though it would be his last.

"Excuses?" Hagen inquired sharply.

Seton knew what excuses were worth. "No, sir."

"Then draw your pay."

Seton left.

In general, Hagen was rarely hard on the people under his control. Manipulative, yes, but not unfair. However, he was in a bad mood, and had been for some time now. His plans were in disarray, he had just been passed over for the position of director of the FBI, and his small agency had suffered a number of losses in manpower over the past two years. In fact, he had lost his two best agents, and those people he had occasionally borrowed from other agencies had suddenly become unavailable to him.

And, worst of all, Hagen's greatest plan seemed to be in ruins about his ears. His idea—brilliant, he had thought—had been to fake a kidnapping of Josh Long, an exceedingly wealthy and powerful man, for the express purpose of sending Long's impressive security force, his very talented wife, one of Hagen's former agents, and his friends after the man Hagen had intended to implicate in the kidnapping—an international terrorist known simply as Adrian.

Adrian, once leader of the terrorist group called the Final Legion, was the single criminal Hagen had gone after but not succeeded in capturing. The failure was a raw wound to his vanity.

His plan would have worked, Hagen knew. Raven Long had been one of Hagen's best agents, and the people surrounding her and her husband were a highly talented group perfectly capable of tracking down Adrian and capturing him. It would have worked. But Hagen had been forced to be extremely careful, because all those people had strongly developed survival instincts. And he had been forced to employ agents who were not the best.

Josh Long, born and bred in a world where his great wealth and power made him a constant target, had very good instincts indeed. Somehow, he had realized another attempt was about to be made. He and the key men on his team had vanished weeks ago, leaving no trail, and leaving Hagen hamstrung.

And things had gone from bad to worse. Seton, a new agent, had botched his job, and Hagen had to assume the idiot had left fingerprints. Raven would waste no time in having those checked out. And she could. Long Enterprises had the best nonofficial information network Hagen had ever seen. She would get Seton's name within hours. Hagen's only comfort was that Seton's name had not been linked in any way with his own.

Small comfort.

He was left waiting for something to happen, and Hagen hated waiting. He was also uneasily aware that, for the first time in his checkered career, he might well have underestimated his prey. He had not hesitated to make use of the talents of Josh Long and members of his group in the past. Of course not a single member of that inner circle had ever been his target. And, though he had often misled one or the other of them, they had clearly understood his motives.

This time, he doubted they would.

Hagen had always been the dog; never the fox. He had never even considered the feelings of that hunted creature.

Now, he did.

One

Jennifer Chantry wandered casually down the hallway, smiling at the occasional person she encountered without seeing anything but a jumble of facial features. She had spotted at least half a dozen plainclothes security men, and her heart was pounding frantically beneath her calm facade. How on earth was she going to get herself out of this mess? The bracelet was cutting into her palm as her fingers held it tightly. She should have gone to the cloakroom instantly and put it into her small clutch purse, but that would be the first place one would search.

She saw one of the security men at the end of the hall, and felt hunted. It was a strange, unsettling feeling. There was a set of double doors to her left, and she opened one of them and slipped into the room, hoping desperately that the action didn't reflect her wild desire to run.

The room was a study, with floor-to-ceiling bookshelves and a big mahogany desk, a few chairs, and reading lamps. To Jennifer, the room was achingly familiar. It made her throat hurt, and she blinked back sudden tears.

A lamp burned softly at the desk, Jennifer noted before realizing that the room was also occupied by a total stranger. Quickly, she murmured a vague apology and turned toward the door, but then went still.

The door handle was turning slowly, stealthily, and her heart lodged in her throat. Someone had seen her. And Garrett Kelly would just *love* to call the police, and they'd put handcuffs on her, and—

She heard no footsteps, but the big man who had been standing behind the desk crossed the room quickly and, reaching her, unhesitatingly pulled her into his arms.

"Sorry about this," he whispered cheerfully, just before his lips captured hers.

Too astonished to struggle in the first instant, Jennifer was only dimly aware of the door opening, and then softly closing again. She felt the fine material of his cream-colored tuxedo beneath her fingers, felt powerful arms and a hard chest, and long legs pressed to her own. And she felt an instant, helpless response uncurl in the pit of her belly, spreading throughout her body in heated ripples.

"On the other hand," he murmured when he at last raised his head, "I'm not sorry at all. Hello."

Jennifer stared up at him dazedly and, even in bewilderment, felt her heart catch. Good heavens, the man was *beautiful*. Violet eyes lit from within, a strong, handsome face, a smile to make a woman forget her very name.

6

She cleared her throat in a small, bemused sound. "Hello."

His eyes laughed down at her.

Jennifer made a determined effort. "Let go of me," she ordered in a voice better suited to calling kittens.

"Do I have to?" he asked solemnly.

She thought about it, then hastily got a grip on herself. "Yes, of course. Let go of me!"

"Your wish is my command, ma'am," he said, stepping back and raising her hand to his lips with a graceful half bow.

Jennifer hadn't thought there was a man left alive who could say things like that and kiss a woman's hand, but this man did it awfully well. And then he smoothly removed the bracelet from her nerveless fingers.

"Give that back," she gasped, anger and panic warring inside her.

He was holding the bracelet up to take advantage of the faint light, looking at it through suddenly narrowed eyes. "What have we here?" he murmured.

"It's mine!"

"Hush," he warned absently. "You want to have the security people bursting in here?"

It was the last thing in the world Jennifer wanted, and she quickly lowered her voice to a whisper. "Give me the bracelet," she insisted.

He looked down at her, his lips curving in that incredible smile. "It isn't considered very polite to rob your host," he told her gently.

Jennifer bit her lip. "I didn't—I mean, it's . . . Oh, you wouldn't understand!"

"You're undoubtedly wrong about that," he murmured.

"But since I'm on a tight schedule, I don't have the time to insist. How were you planning to get the bracelet out of the house?"

She blinked up at him. "Umm. My purse."

He was shaking his head. "First place they'll look."

"Well, I thought that, but—" Jennifer blinked again. "Please give me the bracelet!"

He eyed her ruby gown thoughtfully. "Are you wearing garters, by any chance?"

"Am I what?" she managed faintly.

"Garters. Those sexy little devices from bygone days used to hold up stockings? They came before some total moron invented pantyhose."

Fascinated, she stared at him. "Yes, as a matter of fact, I am. Why?"

"I love Southern women." Abruptly, he went down on one knee and swept her clinging skirt up above her knees. "Great legs," he told her.

She stared down at his dark head and felt carried along by an irresistible force beyond her power to stop. "Thank you," she murmured.

"Hold the skirt up," he instructed briskly.

Meekly, Jennifer held the skirt up. She could feel his warm fingers on her thigh, then the cooler metal of the bracelet. He was fastening the bracelet to her garter, she realized in astonishment.

He rose easily to his feet and stepped back, frowning slightly as he gazed at his handiwork. "Drop the skirt, and let's see how that looks," he instructed.

Jennifer obeyed.

He nodded in satisfaction. "Fine. No one should notice it under the skirt. Unless our host decides to search his guests, you should get it out all right."

Wondering if she had tumbled through Alice's mirror by accident, Jennifer stared at him. "You aren't going to try to stop me? Or tell security about this?"

He crossed his arms over his broad chest, violet eyes laughing again. "Well, that might be a trifle awkward, you see."

After a baffled moment, she looked past him, remembering where and how he'd been standing when she'd first seen him. "You were at the safe," she said slowly. "Trying to open it."

"Not at all. I'd just closed it. And since I don't want anyone checking for missing valuables . . . Well, you understand."

"You're a thief," she said wonderingly.

Lifting one flying brow, he said in a pained tone, "Now, that's the pot calling the kettle black."

"I'm not a thief!" Jennifer shook her head. "Oh, never mind. I'm leaving."

If she had expected this very peculiar man to try and stop her, she was disappointed. But when he spoke just as she was about to open the door, his words caught her off guard.

"Mind telling me your name?"

"Yes, I do mind," she snapped softly.

"That's all right," he told her, unperturbed. "I'll find out what it is."

She looked back at him, frowning. "Why? To report me later?"

"No. But I've got to hear the story of the bracelet." Before she could respond, he added musingly, "Besides, I definitely fell in love with your legs."

Jennifer escaped while she could, unnerved to hear the sound of soft, deep laughter behind her.

With no security guards in sight, she took a familiar route through the house, making her way carefully and silently along deserted service corridors and small, unused rooms, until she left the house the way she'd come. The room was a small parlor, the furniture draped in dust sheets, and Jennifer went out through a window with a broken lock.

She was in the side garden, an area that had once been beautiful but was now overgrown, and she thought with a pang what a difference a few years could make. She slipped along the almost invisible path, holding her skirt up, all her senses straining for any sound. Carefully, she worked her way around the house and back to the front, skirting the parked cars and keeping her distance from the front entrance.

She paused at the top of the driveway, looking down the long lane that was flanked by tall oak trees dangling Spanish moss. Then she looked back at the house, biting her lip. Who *was* that man? Was he going to be trouble? He was there for some nefarious purpose of his own, certainly, and a large part of her cheered him on if it meant any loss to Garrett Kelly. At the same time, she hardly wanted the house looted of its treasures.

And she couldn't help wondering if that strange man really meant to find her—either because he wanted to be told the story of the bracelet, or because he'd fallen in love with her legs. In either case, the potential for trouble was great.

Still holding her skirt up, Jennifer hurried along the very dark lane, and softly muttered, "Mother, you've really done it this time!"

•   •   •

Some ten minutes later, Dane Prescott rejoined his companion for the evening in the crowded ballroom downstairs. He neatly took her away from two slightly inebriated and adoring gentlemen, neither of whom felt able to fight for her.

"You're better than a Doberman," Raven Long told him admiringly, accepting his arm and beginning to stroll with him toward one of the many hallways the party had spilled into. "One look at you and troublesome men suddenly feel a daunting lack of muscles."

He looked down at her in amusement. "Does that include your husband?"

"My husband isn't troublesome," she reminded him. "And I've never noticed a lack of muscles."

"Neither have I," Dane said with some feeling.

Two pairs of violet eyes met, and Raven laughed. "Did he make that strong an impression?"

"I'll say. You'd expect a business tycoon to be old and crusty, or at the very least young and flabby. Josh looks like he works for a living, and then works out for fun. And I'd hate to get him mad."

"Somebody else did that," Raven pointed out. "And they got me mad too. I don't like it when some faceless enemy tries to get at my husband. And that, in case you've forgotten, is why you and I are attending this party." Her musical voice never changed expression as she asked lightly, "Find anything?"

Dane was leading her down a long, well-lighted hallway that served as a portrait gallery. He stopped at her question, looking at the painting nearest them for a moment, then glancing around to make certain they were alone.

"I was interrupted," he told her, "but I did find something interesting. And not what I expected to find. I'll tell you about that later."

Raven frowned a little, but accepted his enigmatic words. "Who interrupted you?"

Leaning a shoulder against the wall beside the painting, Dane crossed his arms over his chest. "A lady with a stolen bracelet in one hand."

"Somebody else planned to burgle the place tonight?"

"No. I don't think that was it. I didn't have much time to talk to her, but she didn't strike me as a thief."

Raven began to look amused. "You two hit it off, huh?"

"She looked scared. So I helped her hide the bracelet."

"Should I ask where?"

"I wrapped it around one of her garters."

After a blink, Raven said, "Oh. You certainly had an interesting interlude in the study."

"Bear with me." Dane smiled. "I think we've stumbled into a mystery here. Thing is, I don't know if it'll help us find what we're after."

"I'm listening."

Dane brooded for a moment, then began speaking softly but rapidly. "First of all, I think the young lady crashed this party; I can't be sure, but my instinct says yes. I noticed her earlier, and she was jumpy as hell. Second, the gown she was wearing, though it was beautiful and suited her well, was about ten years out of date, and had been recently altered. The garters she was wearing were made of very old lace, not elastic."

Raven nodded slowly. "So she's possibly from a family that was once very well off, but isn't now."

"That was my reading. And she moved the way Kyle does," he said, referring to one of Raven's close friends.

Beginning to look even more interested, Raven said, "That expensive private school look. Every inch the lady."

"Right. Now, all this in itself doesn't mean much—at least probably not to us. But there were a couple of other things. She knew there was a safe behind the desk, even though I'd put the painting back in place before she came in. I implied I was in the room with dishonest intentions; she immediately looked at the safe and suggested I'd been trying to open it. And I recognized her."

"Who is she?"

"I don't know her name yet, but she's the living image of the woman in this portrait." Dane nodded toward the painting they were standing in front of.

Raven turned her head to study the painting, her eyes widening a bit. It was the portrait of a young woman done just after the turn of the century. The woman's gown was a soft rose color with a modest neckline and tightly cinched waist. She held a single pink rose in slender white hands, and wore no jewelry. Her hair was golden, her eyes a clear blue, and there was a look of mischief behind her half smile.

"She's lovely." Raven looked at the brass nameplate attached to the ornate frame, and read aloud, "Jennifer Louise Chantry."

"I checked the other paintings a few minutes ago," Dane told her. "The majority of these *family* portraits are Chantrys. Garrett Kelly, unless through a female line, doesn't have an ancestor to boast of on these walls."

"So why does he own the house?"

"That's what I was wondering. Granted, a lot of these

old Southern places have changed hands a number of times, but it doesn't feel right to me."

Raven was silent for a moment, then asked, "What's your feeling about the girl in the study?"

"I think she was taking back something of hers."

"Kelly's a compulsive gambler," Raven reminded him. "Maybe she lost it to him."

"He won't play cards with women," Dane said flatly.

After a moment, Raven shook her head. "As you said, I don't see that this helps us. At the same time, all we have to go on is that Kelly's head of security tested our defenses at least once. We knew somebody was trying to get at Josh, and during that attempt a couple of weeks ago, he left a nice, clear thumbprint on the apartment's electronic lock. Clumsy, to say the least."

"I suppose there's no question about the print's being Brady Seton's?"

"None. Zach triple-checked. No criminal record, but Seton was in the military, and his prints are on file. His last known, and present, employer is Garrett Kelly."

"How about a little icing on the cake?" Dane said dryly.

"What?"

"In Kelly's safe, I found, and removed, one half of a set of plates used to counterfeit one-hundred-dollar bills. And it wasn't made by an amateur."

Raven's eyes widened, then narrowed. "Curiouser and curiouser," she murmured.

"I'll say. Aside from his gambling, Kelly doesn't have a smear anywhere on his name. Not even an unpaid parking ticket. So what's he doing with a counterfeit plate? And where's the other one?"

"And how, if at all, does it tie up with an attempt to get at Josh?"

"Beats the hell out of me," Dane confessed. "But I have to admit I'm intrigued."

A bit restlessly, she said, "Damn, I wish I didn't have to fly back to New York first thing tomorrow."

"The whole point of your being here tonight," he reminded her, "was to find out if this lead was worth pursuing. I'd say it's a definite yes. I'm in now; Kelly's already invited me to one of his pseudosecret card games tomorrow night. We agreed from the beginning it'd be best to let me work this joker."

"I know. But I really hate leaving you alone down here with no backup. If Kelly's counterfeiting on any scale at all, then he's into some pretty big stakes. It could turn out to be a real mess, Dane."

He hesitated, then smiled. "Well, I won't exactly be alone. Remember that friend of mine who helped us out down in Florida a few weeks ago?"

"The one we never saw?" she asked.

"That's the man."

"He's here?"

"Close. And he . . . um, knows a bit about counterfeit plates and the like."

"You know, I always suspected you wore more than one hat, pal."

"Who, me?"

She didn't push it. "Just tell me this friend of yours is a good backup, that's all."

"Rock solid."

Raven sighed, then shrugged. "I don't like it, but there's nothing I can do at the moment. We've had two near-leaks since Josh and the guys vanished from the public eye. If anyone finds out the head of Long Enterprises has disappeared, then a number of stocks are going to go into tailspins. I have to get back and hold down the fort."

"You could be a drawback here anyway," Dane reminded her. "If Kelly *is* behind the attempt to get to Josh, and if he finds out who you are, our hand's tipped for sure."

She nodded reluctantly. "I know, I know. And you're the best man for this job."

"Thank you." Dane was obviously moved.

"Unless," she added gently, "you get distracted by stray blondes with stolen bracelets."

"I'm a professional," he protested in a wounded tone.

Raven's violet eyes gleamed. "Yes, I know." Then, as she began turning away, she added with amusement, "It's just that I've always wondered what, exactly, your profession *is*."

Dane whistled "Waltzing Matilda" under his breath and didn't respond. Not that Raven expected a response of a different sort. If she'd learned anything in her years as a federal agent, it was not to ask too many questions.

It was often safer not to know.

"Jennifer!" The accent was still thick after nearly thirty years on this side of the Atlantic, but tended to pass almost unnoticed in Louisiana, where both French and Spanish influence had been felt so heavily. But anyone who spent more than ten minutes with Francesca Maria Modesta Lorenzo Chantry realized she was Italian to her bones.

She was a tall woman, still beautiful in her fifties, with coal black hair and flashing black eyes, a husky voice that could switch from madonna to shrew in an instant, and a voluptuous figure that never failed to turn heads. And she embodied every volatile trait attributed to her hot-blooded ancestors.

Jennifer had often wondered if her mother did that deliberately, but since her own cool blond surface concealed a number of volatile traits she could only have inherited from Francesca, she had eventually recognized the truth. The mercurial temperament was perfectly real; it was just that Francesca enjoyed a dramatic nature to boot.

"Jennifer, the bracelet?"

Moving into the tiny living room of their small house about two miles from the plantation, Jennifer collapsed into a somewhat shabby chair and hauled her skirt up. Unfastening the bracelet from her garter, she said sternly, "Mother, you've *got* to stop doing things like this!"

Ignoring the command, Francesca watched curiously. "Why did you put it there?"

"Because it was the only way I could think of to get it safely out of the house." It was impossible to tell her mother the truth, Jennifer reflected.

Her mother laughed infectiously. "So smart, my baby! Oh, my bracelet, my bracelet!"

Jennifer handed it over, sighing. Useless to try to persuade her mother that what she had done was wrong—especially since it was perfectly understandable. Taking one's own belongings back, Francesca would declare, was not stealing. And Jennifer knew her own arguments would lack force for the very reason that she was half Italian herself, and she understood.

Francesca clasped the diamond bracelet around her slim wrist and held it out admiringly. Then, in one of her lightning changes of mood, her sparkling eyes filled with tears. "Your father gave this to me as a betrothal present, my baby. He put it on me with his own hands. That horrible man has no right to it, no right at all! He must be punished, Jennifer!"

"I know, Mother." She brooded about that, forgetting, for the moment, the events of tonight. "If we could just prove he cheated in that card game. I know he did, I *know* it. But none of the others saw him cheat. And Daddy signed over the plantation. What else could he do?"

"A duel," Francesca declared. "My Rufus should have challenged him to a duel." Then, obviously deciding she was being overly critical of her adored late husband, she added magnanimously, "But he was ill, my poor darling."

He had been dying, in fact, though neither Jennifer nor her mother had known that four years ago. Losing his family's plantation, Belle Retour, had been more than his overstrained heart could bear. He had died two months later.

And Garrett Kelly had taken possession of the house immediately after the funeral.

The small house Jennifer and her mother now occupied was, in a sense, a part of Belle Retour. Like most huge old estates, the plantation had suffered runs of bad luck in the past, requiring that parcels of land be sold off from time to time. This small house had been built twenty years before on a ten-acre parcel that had been sold to a cousin. When the cousin had died and willed the house and land back to Rufus Chantry, Jennifer's father had deeded the place to her.

She had used it during her teen years as a studio, where she had worked on her dream of becoming a great artist. In the years between high school and college, Jennifer had faced reality. She was a good artist, but not a great one. Reluctantly giving up her dream, she settled for being a commercial artist.

Now she and her mother lived in the house, and Jennifer more or less supported them both with her work. Her father had been insured, though little of that money was left now. Jennifer and her mother lived comfortably. But neither had ever been reconciled to Kelly's possession of Belle Retour, and neither had given up the determination to get their plantation back.

"I should not have taken the bracelet," Francesca said suddenly.

Jennifer looked at her warily. Such statements from her mother rarely indicated a sense of guilt. "You shouldn't have?" she inquired in a careful tone.

"No. I should have taken one of your father's guns from the cabinet in the study," Francesca decided. Her black eyes snapped. "Yes! Then I could shoot that bastard."

Jennifer winced, but more because she remembered what had been going on in the study tonight than out of any real dismay at her mother's words. Long experience with Francesca's way of reasoning made her appeal to her mother's maternal feelings rather than her good sense. "You'd be arrested for murder, and I'd be all alone. Do you really want that?"

"My baby!" Francesca sat on the arm of her daughter's chair and hugged her tempestuously. "Of course, I would never abandon my baby—even to shoot that man in the heart. But we must get our Belle back, Jennifer. We must!"

"We will," Jennifer assured her. "I've promised you that, Mother."

"*Vendetta.*"

"Well, the American version, anyway."

Francesca looked at her suspiciously. "You sound like your father, my baby. How can you wish for less than that despicable man's blood? He killed your father and stole our home!"

Jennifer didn't deny the accusations, even though she could have pointed out that no one had forced Rufus Chantry at gunpoint to play poker, much less to put up the deed of Belle Retour when he had lost practically everything else. She had loved her father, but gambling had been his weakness and she knew it too well.

"We'll get even with Kelly, Mother. And we'll get Belle away from him. I promise. Just please promise me that you won't do anything yourself. I have to come up with a plan, and if you try to steal, I mean *take* anything else out of the house, it'll just make it more complicated for me."

Francesca looked doubtful. "If you say so, but I cannot wait much longer for revenge."

Much later, as she lay in her small bedroom and stared at the dark ceiling, Jennifer accepted the fact that she was now on a deadline. Her mother's patience these last years had indeed been remarkable, and due partly to the fact that she and her daughter had gone to Italy to spend months with her family after the death of Rufus. A return to her native land had re-minded Francesca of just who and what she was.

She was Italian, and her family was known for at least one vendetta that had lasted half a century. So Francesca would be content to wait for her revenge—as long as she was sure she would get it.

Jennifer was half Italian, and though the years in expensive schools had added a ladylike polish to her cool blond looks, under the surface her mother's blood ran strong in her. And without the calming influence of her father, who had been quite adept at handling the tempests of Latin temper and impulsiveness, Jennifer knew she was apt to be reckless.

But she *wanted* revenge, and no amount of sensible thought had changed that. She wanted her home back, she wanted to prove Garrett Kelly a thief and a cheat, and she wanted to keep her mother out of it if at all possible.

Which was why, of course, she had crashed the party at Belle Retour tonight in search of her wayward mother. And thank God she had found her before Kelly knew either of them was there.

Remembering that, Jennifer suddenly recalled the big stranger with the laughing violet eyes. A thief? What had he taken from the safe? Who was he? She remembered his kiss, and shivered suddenly, unsettled.

Just a stranger, of course, and she wasn't likely to see him again. Still, she couldn't help wondering what he had taken from the safe. . . .

Two

In a large hotel on the outskirts of Lake Charles, Dane Prescott turned from the window of his sitting room and lifted a questioning brow at the man seated on the couch. "Well?"

"It's a beauty all right." The man was turning a counterfeit plate over in his hands. "Someone with real talent made this. And you took it out of Kelly's safe?"

"Yeah. I've never heard a whisper of his name connected with counterfeiting operations; how about you, Skye?"

"No. But it wouldn't be the first time a pristine reputation covered something dirty." He looked up suddenly. "Or the opposite. You did say Raven had gone back to New York?"

"First thing this morning." Dane smiled. "She knows you're here backing me up, but she doesn't know who you are."

Skye shook his head. "We've been running this scam

for too many years," he said. "It can't go on forever. I figure our time's running out."

"Probably," Dane agreed. "We'll have to see if we can pull it off one more time. This is a case that demands both of us work on it. I can get into Kelly's house, I may even be able to look around a little, but if we're going to tie Kelly to a counterfeiting operation, we'll need more than the plate. If he's printing money himself, where's the press? How's he passing the fake money?"

"His infamous poker games?" Skye suggested.

"Maybe. I may have that answered by tonight. We've got to nail it down, though."

"Agreed." Skye looked thoughtful. "By the way, I've got the answers to those questions you called in last night. Belle Retour is owned by Kelly, legally. It was officially listed as a transfer for 'debts owed.' For that, you can read poker losses."

"He won the plantation?"

"Four years ago, from Rufus Chantry. The place had been in his family for two hundred years. Chantry was apparently a compulsive gambler, or at least close to it. He lost the plantation and everything else he owned in a single high-stakes poker game. Two months later, he died of a heart attack. He left behind a widow who wasn't allowed to take anything but her clothes out of the house, and a daughter who was in college at the time."

Dane was looking very intent. "A daughter?"

"Yeah. Your guess about the portrait was on target. Jennifer Louise Chantry is the great-granddaughter of the woman in the painting. She's twenty-six, a commercial artist, and lives with her mother in a small house that was once a part of Belle Retour. Her father deeded it to her on her sixteenth birthday, apparently for a studio."

After a moment, Dane said reflectively, "I don't think I like Garrett Kelly very much."

"He was certainly a dyed-in-the-wool bastard about the plantation. Mrs. Chantry, who's *very* Italian, by the way, wasn't even allowed to take her jewelry. Kelly maintained that every last rock was part of the 'house and contents' signed over to him by Chantry, and the law backed him up because the insurance inventory of jewelry listed everything as a part of the *family* property rather than Chantry's personal belongings, assigned historical value."

"I'm surprised she didn't sue him on that one," Dane commented, frowning.

"I bet she wanted to. Word has it she's a combustible lady. She didn't go to court over it, though, and I couldn't find out whose idea that was." Skye rubbed his nose, suddenly amused. "I managed to get a bit of gossip from some of the locals this morning. It seems most everyone in the area has been waiting, with baited breath, for Mrs. Chantry either to haul off and deck Kelly, or else to stab him when he isn't looking."

Dane lifted an eyebrow. "She's that Italian, huh?"

"In spades. And people around these parts figure she's waited as long as she can stand it to get even." Skye grinned. "We're sitting on a powder keg here."

"Maybe. But I'm not willing to pull out. How about you?"

"Oh, I'm game."

"Good." Dane went over to the compact bar to fix two

drinks, then carried them to the couch and sat down. Handing one to Skye, he said thoughtfully, "We have to find out about that security man of Kelly's, Brady Seton, and if Kelly gave him orders to try and get to Josh Long. If so, why? What's his game? We also have to find out what Kelly's doing with a counterfeit plate, if he's running a press somewhere, if he's passing the money and how, and if he's on his own."

"Tall order," Skye commented.

Dane nodded, but said, "The counterfeiting business first, I think. If we can get Kelly tied to that, it'll give us a lever to find out what his interest is in Josh Long."

"So what's your plan?"

With a wry laugh, Dane replied, "To do what we do best, of course."

Jennifer tried to concentrate on the advertising layout she was working on, but her mind wandered. She looked around the tiny extra bedroom that had become her studio without really seeing it. *Vendetta.* Her mother meant the word in its fullest sense: a blood feud, an all-out, hell-for-leather taking of revenge, no matter what the cost.

The problem was, a part of Jennifer wanted that as well. She tried to temper the desire, assuring herself that no blood need be spilled, that just getting the plantation back would be enough. But the few times she'd seen Garrett Kelly she had been unsettled by the powerful urge to leap at him and scratch his eyes out.

Her mother would have approved wholeheartedly.

Jennifer wanted to get even, but she didn't know *how.* All her efforts to prove Kelly had cheated in the poker game had come to nothing. Her father had signed over the deed before reputable witnesses; the law was on Kelly's side. And though Francesca periodically accused the man of being the worst kind of crook, Jennifer hadn't been able to find evidence that he was anything but a model citizen with a taste for private gambling.

Vaguely, she was aware of the doorbell ringing. She just didn't know—

"How dare you!"

She heard those words from her mother and leaped up, hurried out of her studio, down the hall and toward the front door. That particular tone in her mother's voice was reserved for Garrett Kelly, and if that man had dared to come here, her mother was perfectly capable of killing him.

She stopped at the end of the hallway, knowing she couldn't be seen by whoever was outside, while she could see clearly. Francesca had the front door blocked with her stiff body, every angle showing proud outrage. And Kelly's angry voice was perfectly audible to Jennifer.

"You were both there last night, and don't deny it! But I'm prepared to be generous. I won't press charges against you, but I will have my property returned."

"Your property?" Francesca's voice rose to a magnificent soprano, steady as a rock. "You soulless cur, the bracelet is my property! Mine, do you hear? My dear husband gave it to me, and I will not see it in your hands!"

"Bracelet?" Kelly sounded surprised, but his voice quickly hardened again. "I don't give a damn about any bracelet. I just want what you took from my safe."

"Your safe? It is not *your* safe! It is my *husband's*

safe, *my* safe, and my *daughter's* safe! It is our house! You stole it from us, you thieving son of a—"

"Oh, for God's sake!" Kelly exploded. "Where's your daughter? Maybe she knows how to talk sense."

Francesca drew herself up even more stiffly, and her voice dropped suddenly, even and deadly. "You will not touch my baby. You will not enter our house. If you come near us again, I will cut your heart out."

After a long silence, Kelly said furiously, "This isn't over. I'll get my property back."

"No," Francesca told him gently. "*We* will get *our* property back." She stepped back and slammed the door, locking it with an audible click.

"Mother?" Jennifer moved forward, shaken by the hatred—and the danger—she had heard in Kelly's voice.

Her mother turned to her, perfectly calm, and held out a small ruby clutch purse. "You left this at the house last night."

"I'd forgotten all about it." Jennifer took the purse. "No wonder he knew we'd been there. I drove the car partway, so I took my license."

"He's a horrible worm," Francesca said. But she sounded content, and Jennifer knew it was because her mother had definitely enjoyed the confrontation.

But Jennifer was worried. She hadn't liked the sound of Kelly's voice; he had sounded both enraged and, curiously, panicky. It was hardly a stable combination. Realizing suddenly, she said slowly, "What could have been taken from his safe? That other man . . . perhaps he . . ."

"What man?" her mother asked curiously.

"Someone at the party." Jennifer's voice was absent.

"And he said something about not wanting anyone to search for missing valuables. But, what was it?"

"I took nothing that did not belong to me," Francesca stated virtuously.

Jennifer nodded, again absently. "Yes. Mother, I need to make a few calls, then I may have to drive into town."

"Fine, my baby. I shall read a book. And tonight, we will have a celebration because I drove that worm from our door."

Almost wincing, Jennifer reflected that her mother's celebrations tended to be hard on the stomach. Italian or not, Francesca couldn't cook—but refused to stop trying. Still, culinary pursuits kept her mother happily occupied, and Jennifer was willing to put up with whatever was necessary to keep her happy.

Returning to her studio, Jennifer called a familiar number and smiled as a bright voice answered.

"Jennifer! I saw you at the party last night. It's a good thing that Kelly person was busy with his poker game in the back parlor. What on earth were you doing there?"

"Guarding the family silver, Sharon," Jennifer replied lightly.

"Oh, I've been doing that for you, sweetie. Why else would I go to that awful man's parties?"

Sharon LaCoss had been Jennifer's best friend all through school, and they were still close. Sharon also knew everyone in the area, and she was infamous for her ability not only to spot a stranger in her orbit, but also to find out exactly who the stranger was within hours.

"Sharon, I need your help."

"Just ask," her friend said instantly.

"There was a man at the party I've never seen before. Big, dark, very good looking, and he was wearing a cream-colored tux. I have to talk to him."

"No problem," Sharon said cheerfully. "I'd have had to be blind not to notice that one. He came in with a lovely brunette on his arm; didn't spend too much time with her, though."

Jennifer felt a pang she refused to acknowledge. "Do you know who he is?"

"Rick found out for me," Sharon said, referring to her fiancé of two months. "The guy's name is Dane Prescott, and he's staying at a hotel here in Lake Charles. Seems one of Kelly's poker buddies brought him along to the party and introduced him. He's supposed to be some hotshot gambler from Florida, with a lot of bucks."

"I see."

Sharon's voice wavered between curiosity and teasing. "If you're worried about the brunette, I'd say there's nothing there but friendship. They acted like buddies, not lovers. No romantic spark, you know?"

Jennifer bit back an instinctive denial of interest in Dane Prescott as a man, since the truth was a bit too complicated to go into at the moment. "We'll see. Um . . . exactly where is he staying, Sharon?"

So Sharon told her. Exactly.

The knock on the door caused both men to go still. Skye looked at Dane, and asked softly, "Expecting anyone?"

"No," Dane replied just as softly. "No one."

Skye rose and moved soundlessly across the room

toward the bedroom, carrying the counterfeit plate in one hand, and his drink in the other. "I'll wait in there."

"Right." Dane slid his sketch of Kelly's house off the coffee table and placed it in the top drawer of the desk, then went to the door and looked through the security peephole. He glanced back over his shoulder to make sure the bedroom door was closed, then opened this door and stepped back.

"Hello again, Miss Chantry."

She came into the suite with a determined stride, and Dane could hardly help being amused as he closed the door behind her and followed her into the sitting room. Today, she was wearing jeans and a short-sleeved blouse, her golden hair swept up casually in a ponytail; she looked younger than last night, but just as lovely and considerably less frightened.

He had a vivid memory of the way that ruby gown had clung to her every curve, and his body remembered too well those curves pressed against him.

"What can I do for you?" he asked politely, leaning back against the bar with his arms crossed over his chest.

"Why were you at Belle Retour last night?" she demanded.

"There was a party. You may have noticed."

Her blue eyes took on a glint of anger. "That isn't what I meant, and you know it. What did you take from the safe?"

"Nothing of yours. Or your mother's."

She was silent for a moment, staring at him. How much did he know about her and her mother? A great deal, it seemed. Then, slowly, she said, "You took some-thing of Kelly's. Something important."

Dane raised an eyebrow. "What makes you say that?"

"Because he thinks my mother and I have it. He came to our house a couple of hours ago, demanding we give it back. He threatened my mother. I don't like it when someone threatens my mother." She drew a deep breath. "I'd side with the devil if Kelly were storm-ing hell, but I won't have my mother hurt. So I want to know exactly what you stole from Kelly."

"Damn," Dane muttered, frowning. He hadn't ex-pected Kelly to blame the theft of the plate on anyone specific. Considering how crowded last night's party had been, anyone could have gotten in and out of the study. But it made sense for him to suspect Jennifer and her mother; that safe hadn't been changed in twenty years, so of course they'd know the combination.

"What did you take out of the safe?"

Dane ran a hand around the back of his neck and looked ruefully at her. "I can't answer that, I'm afraid."

"Why not?"

"I'm not in a good position here," he said. "I certainly don't want Kelly to find out I got into his safe. In fact, that's the last thing I want him to know. So why should I blithely tell you what I took out of that safe?"

Jennifer saw his point, but she hadn't come here prepared to take no for an answer. She gritted her teeth. "Word has it you came here to play poker with him. I can tell you right now he won't welcome you if I tell him you were in his study last night, and that you had the safe open."

"What would you gain by doing that?" Dane asked slowly.

"My mother's safety. Kelly's desperate to get back whatever it was you took. And I don't much care who he's after as long as it isn't my mother or me."

"Reasonable," Dane agreed dryly. He studied her for a moment in silence. "The grapevine around here is pretty good. What else have you found out about me?"

"That you're a gambler from Florida with a lot of money to lose. I already knew you were a thief."

"Just like I knew you were a thief."

Jennifer stiffened. "I am not! I just—"

"Appearances," Dane murmured, "can be deceptive. Never assume, Miss Chantry. Or may I call you Jenny?"

She blinked at him, suddenly doubtful. Was he only a gambler and thief—or was he something more? She didn't know, couldn't be sure. "Nobody calls me Jenny," she said at last.

"Then I'll be the only one. Good." Before she could respond, he went on calmly. "I've been listening to the grapevine too. And I heard that both you and your mother want Belle Retour back. Also, I understand that you would dearly love to get your hands on a means for revenge against Kelly."

It was all common knowledge in the area, but Jennifer wasn't happy he knew. "So?"

He drew a breath and let it out slowly. "So, maybe we can work together."

"Why should I trust you?"

"You'll have to decide for yourself about that. All I can tell you is that the prospects are good for Kelly going to jail for a long, long time. And not for cheating at cards."

"For what?"

"First," Dane said calmly, "you have to decide whether you trust me."

"How can I know? Tell me something to convince me."

Dane grinned. "Well, I could tell you that my heart is pure, but I doubt you'd believe me."

Ridiculously, Jennifer felt herself torn between giggling and snorting in disbelief. Oh, this man had charm. Why, she felt she could almost pluck it out of the air, like a raindrop. She steeled herself against the appeal of him, remembering the need for revenge against Kelly, remembering her mother, remembering a "lovely brunette." "You're right. I don't believe you."

He rubbed his nose, looking at her thoughtfully but with those vivid eyes laughing. "I was afraid of that. And I don't suppose swearing on my honor would do any good either?"

"If I don't know whether you're trustworthy," she pointed out, "then why would I believe you *have* any honor?"

He sighed. "That is a point. Look, Jenny, one of us is going to have to trust the other, or we won't get anywhere."

She lifted her chin. "Then you trust me. Since you seem to know so much about my background, you must have guessed that the bracelet I took last night belonged to either me or my mother. It should be fairly obvious that I have every reason in the world to want to get Garrett Kelly. It's *your* reasons that are in doubt here."

Dane sighed again. "All right, dammit. Sit down;

we're going to be here for a while. Would you like a drink, coffee?"

"No, thank you." She sat down a bit gingerly on one end of the long couch, and watched him sit a couple of feet away. And her guard was back up, because something told her this abrupt giving in of his had been expressly designed to win her trust.

Conversationally, he asked, "Do you know that your eyes turn almost gray when you're suddenly having misgivings about something?"

Jennifer blinked. "What?"

"Well, it's obvious you think I'm trying to trick you in some way." He was half turned toward her, one arm along the back of the couch between them. "I'm not that devious, I promise you."

She reserved judgment on that, trying to ignore the beautiful, long-fingered hand so near her shoulder. "Just tell me what this is all about, all right?"

"All right." Carefully, Dane began by saying, "I was asked by a friend to check the contents of Kelly's safe. And, before you ask, what I was looking for had nothing to do with valuables; I wanted to find some paper connection between Kelly and another man. Since that has nothing to do with you, and since it isn't my story anyway, you'll have to take that much on faith."

She accepted that for the moment, but had what seemed to her a pertinent question. "Do your friends often ask you to break into other people's safes?"

Dane was smiling. "Well, let's just say that sometimes my friends need to know things about people, and I happen to be good at getting information."

"By breaking into safes?"

"Whatever it takes."

Jennifer felt baffled. This didn't sound like a garden-variety thief or gambler; but then, how many of those had she met? "All right. For now."

"Suspicious Jenny."

She wasn't sure she liked the way he said that shortened version of her name. It sounded like a caress. "Just finish the story, would you, please?"

"Certainly. I didn't find that paper connection I was looking for in the safe. But I did find a plate used to counterfeit hundred-dollar bills."

She felt her eyes widen. "What?"

"Interesting, isn't it? A fine, upright citizen like Kelly making his own money. If he is, of course."

Jennifer was trying to think clearly. "There's a question about that? I mean, why else would he have this . . . this plate?"

"He could have been holding it for a friend; he could have found it himself and be busy blackmailing someone. You see, Jenny, we need two more items to prove Kelly's making money himself. The other plate, because it takes two to print a bill, and the press to do the printing."

"I see." She mused about that for a moment, then frowned at him. "What's your angle in this?"

"Justice?" he suggested in the tone of a man who didn't expect to be believed.

"Try again."

Dane shrugged. "All right, then. I have a friend in the Treasury Department, and I owe him. After I found the plate last night, I gave him a call. He asked me to try and find those other two items, and to see if I could discover whether Kelly's passing phony money at his poker games. I said I'd do it. I hate debts," he added almost parenthetically.

Those were the first words he'd said that held a ring of truth for Jennifer. She believed him. Her father had been the same way about debts; she wondered idly if it was a trait peculiar to gamblers. "So what're you planning to do?"

"The first thing *we* have to do," he said, "is get the plate back into Kelly's possession without making him suspicious."

"Is that possible?"

"It better be. We have to divert suspicion from you and your mother, and at the same time keep it far away from me. As you pointed out, Kelly would hardly invite me into his house if he found out I'd rifled his safe. And I have to be able to come and go at the house, or we'll never find the evidence to put him away for good."

Jennifer was quiet for a moment, then said, "I don't suppose this is going to get Belle Retour back for mother?"

Dane hesitated. "I don't know. But I have to tell you it's doubtful. The plantation was legally transferred into Kelly's name. Chances are, the property's his no matter what happens. There's a slim chance though, that if he were convicted and the government slapped a hefty fine on him as well as a prison term, he would have to sell Belle Retour to raise the money."

"Couldn't we prove he cheated my father?" Jennifer asked. "A person isn't allowed to profit from crime, and he *did!*"

"That's a sticky point to prove in court when it comes to gambling."

Jennifer had kept her hopes up these last years, convinced that she could do something to restore Belle Retour to the family. Now, for the first time, she realized how impossible a dream that had been. Her home, lost to her. Her promise to her mother, just so many empty words.

"Damn," she whispered. "We can't get it back. We can never get it back."

"Yes, you can," Dane said suddenly. "And you will."

She looked at him, blind for a moment, her eyes full of unexpected tears. "What? How?"

He smiled an odd, crooked smile. "On that point, you'll again have to trust me. But I promise you, Jenny, before this is over, you'll have Belle Retour back."

She didn't believe him. But, at the same time, she realized that her only chance of revenge against Kelly lay in helping to find evidence against him for counterfeiting. If she could do that, it would be enough. It would have to be enough.

"Okay. So what do we do?"

"First, I want you to pay a little visit to Kelly."

"I hate that man," she said.

"Good. Make sure he sees it. You're furious with him. He came to your house and threatened your mother, all because he thought she took something from his safe. Tell him your mother went nowhere near that study, but you saw other people going in and out all evening. Even one of his security men went in at least three times—you saw him."

Jennifer was listening intently. "Why am I pointing at the security guard in particular?"

"He's as good a target as any. Besides, I still have to check on that connection I mentioned. So you be sure and direct Kelly's attention that way. And he'll find the plate hidden in the guard's room."

"How will—Oh. You'll put it there?"

"Right. By the way, since Kelly didn't tell you what had been stolen, be careful not to let on that you know."

"He knows Mother—I got the bracelet."

Dane didn't appear to notice the slip. "Fine. Go on to him about that—that it was just a lousy bracelet, nothing to make such a fuss over. Really give him hell. How's your temper?"

She managed a smile. "I'm half Italian. My temper's a force of nature."

He laughed softly. "Perfect."

"What happens after he finds the plate, assuming he believes me and searches the guard's room?"

"Then I go to work trying to find the other plate and the press. It's very likely that it is somewhere in the house, or nearby."

Jennifer was silent for a moment, then offered, "I could sketch a floor plan for you. It might save time."

Dane rose and went over to the desk, returning with several blank pieces of hotel stationery and a pencil. He sat down—a bit closer this time—and handed them to her. "Thank you, Jenny," he said quietly.

She reached for a large hotel menu on the coffee table and slid it under the papers on her lap, then bent her head and began sketching. "I don't know why I'm trusting you," she muttered, half angry. "You'll probably steal everything but the drapes."

"No, I won't do that."

She sketched for a few moments, but the silence began to bother her. And she could feel his eyes on her, not laughing now but lit from within as always, like candlelight through fine violet china. Like sunlight through purple clouds, after a storm. "Why did you become a gambler?" she asked abruptly.

For the first time Dane found that question difficult to answer. And he knew why. Her father had lost her home gambling; she couldn't have a high opinion of that particular form of "recreation." He knew, in fact, that it was his gambling she mistrusted more than his possible talent at stealing.

"No answer?" she asked dryly.

"I happen to be good at it," he said finally. "I have a great memory and excellent concentration, and I've been playing cards since I was a kid. I'm a *professional* gambler, Jenny. Not a compulsive one."

"Is there a difference?"

He studied her delicate, serious profile, aware suddenly of a jumble of emotions. He didn't want her to believe the worst of him, but he had little choice other than to continue telling her the variety of half-truths he had lived with and protected for more than ten years.

No choice.

"There's a difference," he told her. "I never believe bad luck will turn with the next card; I never believe good luck will last; and I never bet *everything*. Never."

Three

"Are you lucky?" she asked without looking at him.

"Usually."

"Do you cheat?"

The question didn't offend him, not when he knew her own story as well as he did. "I know how," he said steadily. "And I know how to spot others cheating."

"You didn't answer the question."

He couldn't answer with a lie. "I never have. But I suppose I would, if the stakes were high enough."

"What price honor," she murmured.

That did bother Dane, and though there was no sound, he could almost feel Skye move restlessly in the next room as he, too, heard the cut that went deeper than the protective armor of a masquerade. " 'His honor rooted in dishonor,' " Dane said a bit roughly.

Her fingers stilled over the developing sketch, and Jennifer turned her head to look at him. "Tennyson."

Dane half laughed, though it wasn't a sound of amusement. "Yes. If I remember, the next line is, 'And faith unfaithful kept him falsely true.' Paradox."

"Is that what you are?" she asked curiously. "A paradox?"

"I'm a gambler," he said in a flat voice.

After a moment, Jennifer went back to her sketching. She was disturbed. Not by what he had said, but by the way he had looked when he said it. Grim. She got the feeling somehow that he didn't like labeling himself a gambler.

When she finished sketching the house a little later, it had taken a sheet of paper for each floor, and Jennifer handed him the three sheets. "There's a cellar. I've marked the stairs, but it's cluttered wall to wall with two hundred years of storage. The attic's the same way, filled with trunks and boxes."

Dane was studying the floor plans intently. "We'll save those for last, then. Thank you, Jenny. This'll be a great help."

She nodded. "When should I confront Kelly? You'll need time to replace the plate."

"He's invited several other men and myself to dinner tonight before the game; we'll be there by six for drinks. If you could come around six-thirty, that should give me enough time."

Jennifer's slightly puzzled frown cleared. "Oh, I see. You'll slip out while I'm there and put the plate in the guard's room."

"Right," Dane said, though he knew that Skye would most likely do the actual skulking.

She nodded and got to her feet, looking at him a bit warily as he too rose. "All right, then. Will you—is there some way you can let me know what Kelly's reaction is? Later, I mean?"

"Of course. In fact, why don't you meet me on the grounds before you leave."

"But won't Kelly notice you're missing?"

"Not if you rattle him enough. Besides, if he asks, I'll tell him I went out into the garden for some air."

"All right. Where should we meet?"

"You know the place better than I do. You'll have to move your car as if you've left. Anyplace between the house and the road where we aren't likely to be seen."

Jennifer thought briefly. "As you start down the lane toward the road, there's an old, rutted track that leads off to the left. It winds up to the main road. I can pull the car off there, and meet you just inside the woods. You'll be about a hundred yards from the house."

"Good enough." He walked with her to the door, and opened it for her. "We'll get Kelly," he told her.

She looked at him, half puzzled and quite uncertain, then shrugged almost helplessly and left. Dane closed the door behind her and slowly returned to the sitting room.

"A friend in Treasury?" Skye asked in a pained tone.

"Well, I'm bound to have at least one," Dane told him.

"And what was that about promising to get her plantation back for her? Dane, are you out of your mind?"

"Probably. Don't rub it in."

Skye half closed his eyes. "Great."

"There has to be a way to do it," Dane said.

"And you did promise," Skye murmured. "I hate it when you do that. I always end up getting shot at."

"Very funny."

"It's true. You're hidebound about promises; once you make them, you have this uncomfortable habit of doing whatever is necessary to keep them."

"Oh, shut up. I have an idea."

"I was afraid of that."

Jennifer had a restless afternoon. With several hours to kill before her visit to Garrett Kelly, she returned to the house she shared with her mother and went back to work. Or tried to. She couldn't seem to keep her mind off Dane Prescott.

She was intuitive, a trait strengthened by her artistic work, yet she had never felt such a jumble of puzzling, conflicting impressions of a person. Even at that first meeting last night, an interlude she had carefully blocked out of her mind while with him today, Dane had baffled her. Startlingly handsome, with a heartbreaking smile and the most *alive* eyes she'd ever seen, he had been smoothly charming, humorous, and remarkably offhand about her theft of the bracelet and his own larcenous activities. He had held and kissed her, obviously as a ploy to fool the person opening the study door; yet his action, begun in an almost comically polite manner, had changed in those few seconds to something a great deal more personal.

That had been last night. Today there had been a subtle difference in him. Jennifer found it hard to pin down, except to feel certain that she had seen more of him, as if some protective layer of himself had been discarded. He had been more serious, even grave at times, treating her as an intelligent woman rather than taking advantage of her bewilderment as he had last night. He had been obviously disturbed that she and her mother had been blamed for the rifled safe, and quick to suggest a way of repairing that damage.

And after her dig at his honor, Jennifer had seen as well as sensed a reaction she hadn't expected from him. He had felt that cut, and felt it deeply. His quote from Tennyson had held bitterness, and when she looked at him, the light behind his eyes was absent for the first time.

A professional gambler, a thief—and honorable? It seemed impossible, and yet . . . Would a man with no honor give a sweet damn if he were accused of having none? Jennifer didn't think so. But a man who was highly conscious of his personal integrity and who, perhaps, lived a life that all too often tested that integrity might well be sensitive about accusations.

Jennifer had been raised by such a man. Rufus Chantry had been, in many ways, a man out of his time. His instincts had harked back to the days when *gentleman* was more than a word; it was a way of life. Yet his increasing addiction to gambling, stronger every year, had first bent and then finally broken his honor. That was why he signed over his family's home without protest, and why he made both his wife and daughter promise not to try to disturb that "gentlemen's agreement" in open court.

He had staked his home in a card game; he had lost it. Like a gentleman, he paid the debt. It never occurred to him that Kelly might have cheated to win, and the stain he felt on his honor had come, not from having lost the plantation, but from having staked it in the first place.

Jennifer, having been raised by a man with that

old-fashioned, almost extinct kind of integrity, was far more sensitive and understanding of it than most modern women. And she was appreciative of it. It had been her father's strength, just as gambling had been his weakness.

And she was bothered now, because she sensed that same rock-solid core of integrity in Dane. Whether or not he was conscious of it, she believed it existed. It could be something as focused as a personal code of honor, a set of rules and limitations defined by him for his own reasons and having little to do with law or accepted morality. Or it could be something broader and looser, a set of lines he would cross only reluctantly—and, as he had said, if the stakes were high enough.

What price honor, indeed.

Until she discovered Dane's answer to that riddle, she couldn't trust him fully.

"Jennifer! You'll strain your eyes." Francesca came into the room and turned on the lamp over Jennifer's drafting table.

After a hasty glance at her watch, Jennifer relaxed. It was only a little after five. She had forgotten to open the blinds in the room, and since the late afternoon sun was partially blocked by the trees outside it had gotten steadily darker without her noticing.

"You've done no work since you came back," her mother noted, casting a practiced eye over the sheets Jennifer had pinned to the table. "What troubles you?"

Jennifer hesitated, reminding herself of her decision not to tell her mother about the attempt to get evidence against Kelly. It was best not to raise her hopes, and besides, Francesca was all too likely to jump into the situation herself with gleeful recklessness. But she had to say something, so Jennifer again played to her mother's maternal and feminine instincts.

"I was just thinking about that man," she said lightly. "The one I met last night."

Francesca's bright dark eyes became even brighter. She had been trying to get her daughter matched up with a suitable man since her late teens, and had refused to give up hope despite Jennifer's independent nature. "Who is he, my baby? Is he handsome? Can he take care of you properly?"

Jennifer almost laughed, but wondered uneasily if she was creating a monster here. "Mother, I just met him—"

"He is unmarried, is he not?" Francesca demanded suspiciously, her accent thickening as she became more Italian. "You would not become the lover of a married man! Unless he were very rich, of course," she added.

Long accustomed to her mother's slightly nontraditional views of male-female relationships, Jennifer said patiently, "I'm not going to be anybody's lover, rich or not. I told you, Mother, I hardly know the man. All I know is that he doesn't wear a wedding ring."

"Ah! That means nothing; some wives are stupid to allow such nonsense. We must discover if there is a wife."

"And then poison her?" Jennifer murmured.

"Divorce is easier," Francesca said, unmindful of irony.

Jennifer looked at her in amusement. "I thought marriage was forever?" she said, curious to see how her mother would rationalize her rapid dismissal of an inconvenient wife when her oft-stated view was that a wedding ring never came off.

Francesca gave her an intent look. "Well, of course, my baby. When it is right. But, obviously, this woman interferes with your destiny. She must be made to release your man. It will all be arranged—you will see."

Feeling a kind of fascinated horror creep over her, Jennifer hastily closed her mouth and then said a bit desperately, "I don't even know if there *is* a wife! And he isn't my man, Mother. I just think he's . . . interesting, that's all."

"Interesting?" Francesca gave the word four distinct and appalled syllables. "You would use such a pale word to describe this man? He does not cause your blood to run hot through your body? Your heart does not pound at the sound of his voice? You do not melt when he touches you?"

Jennifer closed her mouth again and said rather weakly, "Well, I've hardly been with him long enough to know."

Francesca threw up her hands in a purely Latin gesture of disgust. "I lose all patience with these *modern* men! There is not a real man to be found. Not since your father. Not one knows how to make love to a woman, how to fill her senses with the very essence of himself!"

"Mother . . ." Torn between laughter and astonishment, Jennifer was also coping with the innate shock of an adult daughter confronted by a whole new insight into her parents' relationship.

"And you!" Francesca's eyes were snapping. "I cannot believe I have raised you to be so tame, so—timid. In-ter-es-ting! Is that a feeling of passion, of love? No! Is that a feeling of desperation? No!"

"But, Mother, I—"

"You must feel this for your man! He must fill your senses, your heart, and your soul. He must be everything for you, or he is *not* for you."

"I'm sorry I started this," Jennifer said rather blankly.

Her mother ignored the statement. She reached out suddenly, her nimble fingers plucking the elastic band from Jennifer's ponytail so that her hair fell loosely around her face. "Why do you wear your lovely hair this way? Such a forbidding style! And those horrible trousers—"

"Jeans. Mother, I'm working."

"This man must see the woman you are, my baby. Go and put on a skirt; he must see your legs."

Jennifer suppressed a wild desire to blurt, *He's seen them, and thinks they're great.* "I'm not going to chase after a man to show him my legs, Mother."

But her mother had already nudged her out of the chair and was leading her firmly toward her bedroom. "You must see him, of course, as soon as possible. You must know if he is the one. Discover if there is a wife, for if there is we must remove her at once. Unless he is *not* the one. She may keep him if that is the case."

"Generous of us," Jennifer murmured. She would have continued to protest her mother's determination, but she had seen that steely persistence too often in her life not to know the uselessness of holding back floodwaters with a paper dam. So she obediently changed into a prettier blouse—pale blue with a deep V neckline—and a silky print skirt. She flatly refused to wear hose, compelled by a sudden memory of fingers on garters, and her mother accepted that cheerfully.

Fifteen minutes later, dressed, hair brushed, and filled with a rueful sense of great-oaks-from-little-acorns-grow, Jennifer found herself being almost literally pushed out the front door. She had to leave anyway, since it was time for her confrontation with Garrett Kelly, but she paused a moment to direct a stern command at her mother.

"Don't send out wedding invitations, dammit!"

Unperturbed, Francesca smiled widely and said, "Of course not, my baby. We must first discover if he is the right man for you."

Jennifer sighed. "I'll probably be back in an hour or so."

"That is not enough time," her mother said critically.

Wanting to reply to that, but finding no words to do justice to her thoughts, Jennifer shook her head and went out to her small car. She headed toward Belle Retour, trying to work up a good head of steam for Kelly's sake, but having a difficult time.

Her mother. If there was another woman in the world like Francesca, Jennifer thought, it would be a miracle. Her words might not have been pearls of wisdom, but they were eccentric enough to be marked indelibly on the memory of anyone who heard them. Generally leaning toward the traditional view that marriage, between the right people, of course, was forever, she was still perfectly capable of seeing her beloved daughter as the mistress of a wealthy man. She was firmly convinced that no woman was complete without the adoring attention of a man, whether in or out of wedlock.

Jennifer could have argued that point, having come of age in a world considerably different from that of her mother's generation, and being very American in her attitudes. She had made no attempt to air her own views because of her love for Francesca—and the rueful knowledge that her mother would never accept them, perhaps not even understand.

Jennifer pushed the last of those thoughts out of her mind as she turned the car into the oak-shadowed lane leading to Belle Retour. Angry. She was supposed to be angry. She filled her mind with thoughts of what Kelly had done to her father, to her mother and herself. And she got angry.

She got furious.

In fact, in her zeal to play the role assigned her, Jennifer quite unconsciously abandoned the restraints placed on her since childhood in a variety of expensive private schools. Those schools had imposed their very definite ideas of what a lady should be, and Jennifer had accepted them partly because the discipline needed for control had interested her. She had also cultivated a calm surface because the memories of childhood temper tantrums had convinced her she needed that control.

Now, in a fury, she stopped her car before the house and stormed up to the front door, ignoring the bell because the brass knocker made a more satisfying noise. When the door swung open, she pushed past the surprised butler who had sneaked candy to her as a child, demanding loudly, "Where is he?"

"Miss Jennifer, you shouldn't—"

"I want to see him, Mathews! Where is he?"

"In the parlor, Miss Jennifer, but—"

She didn't wait to be announced. Before Mathews could stop her, she went directly to the closed parlor doors and shoved them open, glaring around the room.

It wasn't a room worthy of a glare, since it was beautiful and spacious; but that didn't placate Jennifer because her own mother had decorated it. She saw men standing and sitting, their heads turned toward the door and their eyes startled. There were six or eight men present, some dressed more casually than others. Various ages, from the early thirties to the mid-sixties. All held drinks in their hands, and she knew most of them if only by name.

Dane was standing by the fireplace with two other men, dressed in a three-piece white suit that made him look peculiarly devilish. His brows were raised in an expression of polite surprise, but his eyes were laughing.

Jennifer's glare didn't pause on him, but swept the room and settled on another man. "I want to talk to you!" she snapped.

Garrett Kelly was a fair man in his fifties, with the profile of a hawk and oddly colorless eyes. He had either been born a gentleman or else cultivated that facade; Jennifer had long ago made up her mind it was the latter. He enjoyed parties and the company of other men with a like taste in gambling, and as far as anyone in these parts could tell, his past was obscure.

"I have guests, Miss Chantry," he said now in his even, toneless, "company" voice.

"Oh, I don't mind them hearing what I have to say," Jennifer told him with biting politeness. "But you might."

After a moment, Kelly glanced around at his guests and murmured, "Excuse me, gentlemen." They nodded and made courteous murmurs, wearing the stiff expressions of people who were intensely curious and trying to hide it.

Jennifer turned and strode back out into the hall,

waiting impatiently while Kelly came out and closed the doors behind them. "My study," he murmured.

"*Your* study," she said bitterly.

"It is mine, like it or not," he told her, leading the way to a secondary hallway on the other side of the house from the parlor. He opened the door of the study and gestured for her to enter, his well-kept hands making a mockery of the courtesy.

She swept past him, head high, having no idea of what, exactly, she was going to say to him, and too furious to care. And before he could even get the door closed behind them, she swung around, making no effort to lower her voice.

"Just what the hell do you mean by accusing my mother of *anything*?" she demanded violently.

In a quieter section of the house, the area reserved for storage and servants, Skye moved silently. It had been a simple matter to find a side window with a rusty latch, and no one had observed his stealthy progress. Jennifer's sketch had been clear enough, and this area of the house had showed the exact location of rooms and small suites set aside for staff.

And the security staff. There were currently two full-time security men on the grounds, a fact Skye knew whether Jennifer was aware of it or not. Her family had worried little about security for the house itself except during social occasions. Kelly, a more paranoid and cynical man than his predecessor, kept his two plain-clothes guards in or close around the house at all times, and hired part-time help during his frequent parties.

Skye had noted the fact that one of the guards seemed assigned to patrol the upper floors; the second guard, Brady Seton, appeared to roam with more freedom, and it was his room Skye was in search of. He moved with no sound, his rubber-soled shoes as soundless on polished wooden floors as they were on carpet; for a big man, he moved like a cat.

He had briefly entered and discounted several rooms in the bare five minutes since he had come in through a window: the butler's suite, the suite occupied by a housekeeper and chauffeur—a married couple—and several apparently unused rooms. He finally located a small suite with two bedrooms that seemed to be the correct ones. The first bedroom he checked held a number of articles belonging to a man, and Skye discounted it when he found a wallet with credit cards in a drawer: this room belonged to the other security man.

In Brady Seton's room, Skye searched quickly and thoroughly out of habit, then drew the counterfeit plate from its hiding place inside his black leather jacket and, after a moment's deliberation, placed it on the top shelf of the closet at the very back against the wall. He cast a professional glance over the seemingly undisturbed room, then turned to leave.

The main door to the sitting room opened with a soft click.

In fluid movement, Skye was against the wall beside the door, a silenced automatic held in his right hand. He listened intently as footsteps moved through the sitting room, but didn't move himself until Brady Seton walked into the bedroom.

"Hello."

Seton turned quickly, a hand reaching toward his

lapel as if to draw the gun nestled under his arm. But he froze, the movement half completed.

"Rotten timing," Skye told him softly.

Seton was an ex-marine, had grown up rough, and knew a variety of self-defense tactics. He had also learned, somewhere along the way, at which moment in a dangerous situation it was wisest to simply give in and think about living another day. This was that moment.

The man he faced was smiling, but Seton trusted that smile the way he would have trusted the polished molars of a shark. His first impression of a big man dressed all in black with a businesslike—and silenced—automatic had been perfectly accurate, and had his impression stopped there he might well have attempted a defensive move. Dangerous men he was accustomed to facing.

But the eyes stopped him cold. They weren't particularly menacing eyes, not cold or hard; they weren't the empty, flat-black eyes of a soulless killer, or the mad eyes of a man beyond the limits of reason. In fact, they were very alive and intelligent eyes. But they were . . . reckless. Careless. They were almost an impudent invitation for Seton to try something.

Try something. Go ahead. And we'll both have a little fun.

Brady Seton didn't move a muscle. He had seen eyes like that before, in the faces of incredibly courageous and lucky men. Men who had led other soldiers into battle, men who had braved burning buildings to rescue trapped occupants. Men whom fate seemed to have touched with a kind of aura, like impenetrable armor.

"Let's have the gun. Carefully."

With extreme and utter caution, Seton handed it over.

Skye stuck the gun inside his belt, then sighed a little ruefully. "You have botched the plan, friend. What am I going to do with you now?"

Seton didn't venture a suggestion.

After a moment, Skye said, "Well. No choice, I'm afraid. Pack a bag—and you're in a hurry, so don't bother to be neat about it."

Seton packed a bag.

For the men who remained in the parlor after Garrett Kelly left, the next quarter of an hour was somewhat uncomfortable. They were all too curious to completely ignore what was going on, especially since they could hear the faint echoes of Jennifer Chantry's voice even through closed doors and sturdy walls. Their own conversations dried up after a few murmured attempts, and they were left contemplating their drinks and each other.

"That one's a shrew," one man finally observed.

"She's got reason," another said, and grinned faintly. "You ought to hear her mother."

"Who is she?" asked one of the few in the room who had no knowledge of the past events.

"She grew up here at Belle Retour," the first man told him. "Her family owned this place for two hundred years, until Garrett won it from her father in a poker game."

"Hell, the stakes better not be that high in tonight's game."

Very conscious of the verbal battle going on several

rooms away, and the presumed activities in another part of the house, Dane said, "The word I got was that Garrett's been on a losing streak. He may have to stake this place trying to recoup his losses."

"I'd rather play for cash," one man said plaintively.

An older man shook his head disapprovingly at Dane's comment. "You should never stake everything unless that's what you're prepared to lose," he said.

Dane smiled slowly. "Isn't that the truth?"

The conversation died away at that point, but when Garrett Kelly reentered the room five minutes later, he didn't seem to notice. They had all heard the slam of the front door and a car roaring away minutes before; he said nothing about that. He was perceptibly distracted, frowning a bit. But his voice remained calm and even when he addressed his guests.

"Dinner will be served in an hour, gentlemen. Please make yourselves at home. I have a few calls to take care of, and then I'll rejoin you."

There were more polite murmurs, following him back out the door.

Dane set his untouched drink aside and said, "I think I'll walk in the garden before dinner." He didn't wait for anyone to offer to join him, but went out through a set of French doors leading onto the veranda.

Four

Dane moved lazily until the overgrown garden hid him completely from anyone in the parlor, then quickened his pace. It was a simple matter to cut through the garden toward the front of the house, and he was easily able to keep out of sight in the wilderness of untended plants and trees while he circled around and headed for the patch of woods to the left of the lane where Jennifer had agreed to meet him.

And she was waiting for him, her small car parked just inside the woods on a rutted track. She wasn't sitting in the car; she was pacing violently beside it.

Dane approached her just a bit warily, intrigued by the sheer unexpectedness of her temper. Granted, she had said that her temper was a force of nature, but her cool blond loveliness and serene grace had painted a rather different—and deceptive—picture.

"Are you married?" she inquired fiercely the instant she caught sight of him.

He blinked, stopping by the car. "No, I'm not."

"My mother wanted me to ask." Jennifer was still pacing, obviously so angry she was hardly paying attention to what she was saying. "I'm glad you're not. Mother probably would have poisoned your wife."

Dane leaned back against her car and folded his arms, patiently waiting for the storm to subside even while thoroughly enjoying the spectacle. "Why would she have done that?" he asked.

"To get her out of the way, of course. She said divorce would be easier, but I know my mother. Poison in the tea, or something. The Borgias were Italian, you know."

"Yes, I remember that." Dane was having a difficult time holding back laughter, but at the same time he was fascinated by what Jennifer seemed to be telling him.

"Then beware," she said darkly, still pacing. "As far as I know, Mother isn't related to them, but you just can't be sure about these things. I can't control her. We'll be lucky if she hasn't already ordered wedding invitations."

"Whose wedding is she planning?" Dane asked.

"Ours," Jennifer snarled. "Damn. And just because I had to say *something* when I hadn't gotten any work done. How was I to know she'd go all maternal and *Italian* on me just because I said I was thinking about a man I'd met? I couldn't have known she'd do that, could I?"

"Definitely not," Dane said solemnly.

"She doesn't even *know* you, and she's probably thinking up names for babies. I've never heard such—Desperation, she said. Passion. Real men, she said, and essences." Jennifer stopped pacing suddenly, an expression of uncertainty passing over her face. "Essences?" she repeated, as if the word sounded odd.

"Sounds fine to me," he offered helpfully.

Jennifer stared at him for a moment, and the doubt vanished to be replaced by a return of her glare. "What price honor?" she demanded intensely.

That one appeared to come straight out of left field, and Dane coped with it in some bewilderment. "Hypothetically?"

"*No*, not hypothetically! You. Your honor. How can I trust you if I don't know that?"

It was, Dane realized, a serious question despite the apparent mental contortions that had brought her to it. Before he could frame an answer, she was going on fiercely.

"Would you sell your honor if the stakes were high enough? How high is high enough? Or is your integrity too important to you? Are there prices you aren't willing to pay, no matter what it costs you? Or do you bet your honesty the way you bet money?"

"*No.*" He hadn't meant the answer to come so harshly, and paused a moment before he continued, looking seriously into her startled eyes. "No, I've never gambled my honor—integrity, self-respect, whatever you want to call it. That price has always been too high to pay. Winning was never so important that I had to bet everything. Losing was never so important that I had to bet everything." He drew a breath. "But I'm a gambler, Jenny. And every gambler knows that sooner or later he'll have to pay—whatever the cost. Even if the price is everything. Even if he staked his honor."

Jennifer stared at him for a long moment, then turned

jerkily away. She was more shaken than she could remember ever having been before. Had that been she, that rambling, fierce woman? God, what she had told him! "I'm sorry," she managed. "I don't know what's wrong with me."

Dane knew. The storm had passed, leaving her a shipwrecked survivor of her own tempest, and reaction was setting in. He straightened away from the car and went to her, but didn't try to make her face him. Instead, he rested his hands gently on her shoulders.

"Why should you be sorry?" he asked.

Stiffly, she said, "Look, just forget everything I've said, all right? I wasn't thinking, and—"

"No, don't do that," he interrupted.

"What?"

"Slip back into your glossy shell." His hands tightened on her shoulders, but his voice remained light. "I didn't realize that's what it was, until you cut loose at Kelly."

"I told you I had a temper."

"And I should have believed you. But that calm surface of yours had me fooled. Is it the Italian blood, do you think, or was your father's family known for their passions?"

She thought his word choice had been deliberate, and it made her uneasy. "My mother takes the credit," she murmured, very conscious of his hands on her. "Or the blame, depending on your point of view. Umm . . . I really should be going."

"Not yet." He turned her to face him, keeping his hands on her shoulders.

Jennifer felt a sense of panic. "All those things I said about my mother and—Well, it's just a misunderstanding, that's all. She's a little volatile, and she just got carried away with the idea—the *wrong* idea—that I was interested in you."

"Is it a wrong idea?"

"Of course it is! I hardly know you."

"I'm very interested in you," he said, and then added thoughtfully, "A tame word, that."

Remembering her mother's opinion of the same word, Jennifer didn't know whether to laugh or swear. "Well, it doesn't matter," she said with a touch of desperation, "because I'm not in the market for a fling at the moment."

"Who said anything about a fling?" He was smiling, violet eyes glowing in that characteristic way, his hands holding her shoulders firmly. "Do you realize that you haven't once said my name?"

Jennifer couldn't break the hold of his gaze. She felt curiously trapped, something alive captured in resin and imprisoned for eons. As if it were some phenomenon she observed apart from herself, she was aware of suddenly quickened heartbeats, of a rising heat that sapped strength, of dizziness. And then her detachment snapped, a rubber band stretched too tightly, and it was *herself* she felt reacting this way, like never before. It was her own body that was unfamiliar.

"How are you *doing* that?" she managed to ask, baffled.

"Doing what? he murmured, the charm of his eyes still holding her, a lure she couldn't resist.

With an effort that left her even more shaken, Jennifer yanked her gaze away, staring fixedly at the open collar of his white shirt. "Never mind. I have to go. Now."

"You sound like a scared little girl, afraid to stop playing dress-up and try the real thing."

Her chin came up in instinctive anger—and her eyes were caught again by his. As unwillingly fascinated as a rabbit watching a circling hawk, she stared into changeable eyes, purple, blue, dark, light, compelling. "Stop that," she said.

"Say my name."

In some part of her mind, Jennifer recognized that his was a conscious ability, and one he was completely aware of. He used it the way another man might use any particular talent, always aware of using it. *Like flipping a switch.* A siren's voice trapped in violet, a visual sorcery. And her instinct was to fight that, to fight him, as if he threatened to take something from her she was unwilling to give. If the lure of his eyes had offered only seduction, she could have fought him; she was both too intelligent and too independent to mindlessly give in to a purely physical demand.

But it was more than that. It was a seduction of the mind as well as the senses, a vivid invitation to fly high and laugh joyously, to *live* on some incredible level she had never even imagined. And it was irresistible.

"Try it," he urged, and he didn't explain if he meant she should stop playing dress-up and sample the real thing, or if the invitation was that other, silent one. Or if both were the same, one appeal to her mind and the other to her heart.

She heard her own voice respond, and it was not a submission but rather understanding and acceptance. "Dane."

"The stakes are high," he warned her softly.

"I know." And she did. A gambler of integrity, Dane

would stake some vital part of himself—but so would she. And in the end, he could win it all.

"Maybe even . . . everything."

Jennifer took a deep breath, a swimmer instinctively treading water to save herself from that third and final plunge in uncertain waters. "I know."

His jaw tightened suddenly as a muscle flexed. "Be sure, Jenny. Be very sure. Once the cards are dealt the game starts."

"Is it a game? Only that?" She was dimly aware that her hands had lifted to rest on his chest.

"Everything's a game, up to a point." He drew her a step closer, his arms slipping around her. "Then it becomes real. The game can't hurt you, Jenny. But the reality can."

Jennifer had never in her life been tempted to stray from the safe and predictable path: school, work, the undemanding social structure of occasional dates meaning little. But Dane's eyes promised so much more. Passion, danger, laughter, pain. The possibilities seemed endless. And the tempestuous nature she had so successfully controlled all these years wanted those possibilities with a wild yearning she had never been conscious of before.

"What happens if I win the game?" she asked finally.

"That depends on what you bet."

"And on what you bet?" When he nodded slowly, she probed, "What are you betting, Dane?"

For a moment, it seemed he wouldn't answer. His face was still, the changeable eyes something else now, something with stronger hints of danger, of a kind of wildness. "Too much," he said in a roughened tone. "Too damned much this time."

When his mouth captured hers, Jennifer again felt that instant response, the uncurling heat inside her. She felt the hardness of his body against her, the unexpected strength of his arms around her. There was nothing lazy about him now, nothing polished or suave or humorous; it was as if another layer of himself had been abandoned. He was rougher, more direct, his growing desire unhidden.

Hers wasn't the only true self hidden inside a "glossy shell," it seemed.

And she could no more resist that than she had been able to stand against the promises in his remarkable eyes. For the first time, she understood her mother's reference to "essences" and how a man could fill a woman's senses with that inner part of himself. Dane was doing that, infusing her somehow with the flickering wildness she had seen in him, igniting her own desires so that they burned brightly.

Her arms slipped up around his neck, fingers tangling in his silky black hair, and she felt his hands slide down over her back, holding her more tightly against him. The stark caress of his tongue half satisfied a terrible craving inside her, just as the feeling of his hard body pressed to her yielding one partially sated the same hunger. But it wasn't enough.

She didn't care that they stood just inside the woods a hundred yards from the childhood home she wanted desperately to be hers again, didn't care that Dane had to go back there, that he would be missed soon. She was no longer questioning trust, or honor, or Dane's enigmatic reasons for being here.

She was luxuriating in sensations. Somehow, perhaps because he was a gambler and a charming, graceful man on the surface, she had expected less physical strength in him despite his size, less power. But beneath the fine cloth of his curiously formal clothing, she could feel the solid muscles of an extremely strong and active man. His grace had become a feline thing, the fluid suppleness of a body under unthinking control. His hands, big and long-fingered, moved over her body with an almost delicate mastery, as if he knew, without a shadow of a doubt, that she belonged to him.

And Jennifer knew it too. Not as a conscious decision, for consciously she would always rebel at the thought of herself as a possession. It was something else, something deeper and more absolute, an acknowledgment that went beyond thought or reason. She was his, no matter what, his by some primitive reckoning they both understood instinctively.

"No," she murmured, an automatic protest against what was, as his lips lifted from hers.

"Yes." He kissed one side of her trembling mouth, then the other, his big body taut against hers. "It's too late now." His voice was deep, husky.

"The game—?" she whispered.

He half laughed, a rough sound that was almost a groan. "Who the hell's talking about a game . . ." His mouth fitted itself over hers again, possessing.

A vague sense of alarm swept through Jennifer, even as her mouth responded to his. No game . . . No game now, so quickly, and no chance of not being hurt if it ended badly. It was real, it was all real, and she had known it would be.

She felt one of his hands in her hair, tangling, holding her head firmly while he plundered her mouth, and a whimper of pleasure and pain escaped her at the force of him. Instantly, he gentled, the fingers in her hair caressing, his lips softening, the hard arms around her cradling.

"Dammit, Jenny," he muttered, lifting his head and staring down at her, "how am I supposed to keep my mind on my job? Why did you have to be the one to walk into the study last night?"

"Of all the gin joints," she managed unsteadily.

He laughed a little. "Right. You had to walk into mine. The lady in red, a stolen bracelet in her hand and panic stirring in her eyes."

"It wasn't stolen," she said idly, fascinated by the way his lips shaped words. "Just taken back."

He kissed her again, eyes restless. "Whatever. You haven't been out of my mind since then. And now I've got to go back into that house and play poker with a shark."

"Do you have to?" She had forgotten everything else, and his words implied that he would soon leave her—an implication she was passionately against.

"Yes." He stifled a sudden groan as she moved against him in protest, her body instinctively seductive, and he slid his hands down to her curved hips, holding her firmly away from him. "Jenny," he warned huskily.

Some part of Jennifer's mind told her to get her splintered control back quickly before she made a total fool of herself, but it was gone, irretrievably cast to the winds. She knew he wanted her and that was enough, for now. "I want you," she told him fiercely.

Dane half closed his eyes, fighting for a command over his body and senses that he hadn't expected to lose, a control he had never before lost. The professional part of him that had always maintained a certain detachment had vanished. He wanted her, right now, here in the woods like some pagan act, their clothes scattered, moss for a bed. He wanted her naked against him, wild in passion, and that need burned in him like a fire almost out of control.

But it was *Jenny* he wanted, the very—what had she said earlier?—the very essence of her, not just a female body matching his in passion. And that desire couldn't be satisfied by a brief and necessarily hurried joining hidden in the woods. He wanted to take her to bed for a week, a month, to learn her so thoroughly that no part of her held a surprise for him—except the surprise of eternal fascination.

"Jenny," he said roughly, "there isn't time."

She went still, gazing up at him as her blue eyes shaded abruptly toward gray. Uncertain. Doubtful.

He framed her face in his hands. "I want you," he told her in a tone that left no doubt of truth. His thumb brushed her trembling lips in a small caress, and he managed a crooked, rueful smile. "But I can't stop other things I've already set in motion. And I won't cheat either of us by trying to fit lovemaking into a schedule."

"Because it isn't a game?" she whispered, very aware of his emphasis on the word *lovemaking.*

"Because it isn't a game," he agreed. "A few days— and then there'll be time for us." His gaze moved restlessly over her face. "Do you understand, Jenny? The other things aren't more important, they're just—more imperative right now."

Though her body still throbbed with unsatisfied desires, Jennifer's mind was at last beginning to clear.

And if a large part of her trusted him implicitly, there was still that rational, reasoning part that distrusted instinct and demanded answers. His discovery of Kelly's counterfeit plates had sounded accidental when he had explained it to her; why was it now so "imperative" that it had to be dealt with on a careful schedule?

Why had he really come here?

"Jenny?"

Her hands had slipped down to rest on his chest, and she unconsciously gripped the lapels of his jacket. "What are you, Dane?" she asked, mystified.

His crooked smile reappeared, and the violet eyes, masked now, were very intent on hers. "A gambler and a thief. You're thinking of hitching your fate to a rogue star, honey. And that's the last warning you'll get from me."

She absorbed that as he took her hand and led her to the car, but when he opened the driver's door she paused, looking at him searchingly. She felt peculiarly displaced, as if some headlong rush had left her quivering on the brink of something, half-committed, still vaguely uncertain. She tried to think, wondering if that were possible right now. "Umm . . . you were going to tell me if I rattled Kelly."

"You did." Dane, too, seemed distracted, but his shuttered eyes never left her face. "He came back into the parlor and then excused himself again immediately. Phone calls to take care of, he said."

"So, he'll look for the plate? And find it in that guard's room?"

"Very likely."

"Then what? The guard will deny taking it."

"Of course, since he's innocent."

"He'll be fired, won't he?"

"Maybe." Dane hated saying that in a hard tone, hated seeing the dismay on her face. Without intending to, he added more gently, "He'll be taken care of, Jenny. I promise. He won't suffer for this."

She relaxed just a bit, clearly trusting him in that. "I—I see. Then what will you do?"

"Play poker." He shrugged. "Find out what's going on. Look for the other press, the plate. Find out if Kelly's passing counterfeit money."

"Because you owe a friend in the Treasury Department?"

"Because I owe a friend."

"Won't Kelly be suspicious when the guard denies everything?" she asked, talking now more for the sake of prolonging their time together than anything else.

"Probably. I'll deal with it, somehow."

Jennifer fell silent. There seemed nothing more to ask, except the one question she wouldn't voice aloud. *When will I see you again?*

"Jenny . . ."

"I know," she said hurriedly. "I have to go."

He reached out to tip her chin up, and leaned over the open car door, kissing her firmly and thoroughly. And that kiss left her in no doubt that desire was still very much present, and still very real.

"Don't forget me," he said softly.

Silently, she got into her car and started it as he closed the door. Then, with a last half-baffled look at him, she drove slowly off down the rutted track toward the main road.

Dane remained there until he could no longer see or hear the car, until the forest swallowed it—and her.

Then he turned slowly and started back toward the house. A glance at his watch told him he still had time before dinner, that the interlude with Jennifer had spanned minutes only.

He wondered if he was being a damned fool.

A soft whistle caught his attention just as he found a way back into the overgrown garden near the side of the house, and he paused, looking around.

"Here," Skye said in a low voice, stepping out from the early evening shadows beneath what might once, in an era of garden parties, have been an arbor.

Dane looked at him for a moment, then glanced around to make certain they were alone. There was no one in sight, no sound to be heard. Joining his partner in the dimness of the arbor, he said in an equally quiet tone, "Taking a chance."

"Couldn't be helped," Skye said. "Mind if I ask you a question?"

"You will anyway," Dane muttered.

"You're so right. When're you going to tell your lady the truth?"

Dane didn't answer for a moment, or look at the other man. Instead, he gazed toward the house, senses automatically probing to alert him in case someone approached. "The truth?" he said finally. "Ten years of lies, shadows, and half-truths. What can I tell her?" Then, realizing, he shot his partner a sharp look. "You saw us out there."

"Sorry. Purely unintentional, I assure you. I was looking for you. And you didn't answer the question."

"Yes, I did."

"Cut it out," Skye said roughly. "You know what I'm talking about."

They stood gazing at each other, two men who had been partners for a decade and best friends much longer than that. Both big men, both with bright eyes and shadows inside. Men whose shared pasts formed a bond rarely put into words. Men who knew each other too well to be able to dissemble; between them, there was little left except the unvarnished truth.

"She talked about honor, Skye," Dane said tautly. "What could I say to that, except more half-truths? What could I tell her? If I have any honor left to me, it's been hacked to pieces over the years."

"That isn't true, and you know it."

"I don't know anything anymore. Except that I am what she thinks I am. A gambler and a thief."

"No. That's the masquerade."

"Is it? When does the actor become the role? We both know it happens sooner or later. Maybe I need Jenny to remind me that I crossed that line a long time ago."

Skye drew a deep breath and released it slowly. "So. You're in love with her."

It hit Dane like a physical blow, a fist driving into him, bruising some integral part of him. But he didn't deny it. Because the unaccustomed tangle of emotions suddenly made sense, and he saw what his partner had seen first.

He was in love with Jennifer. At some moment during the past twenty-four hours, she had become vitally important to him, as necessary as his next breath. He didn't know when it had happened. Perhaps minutes ago, when he had held and kissed her. Or before, when she had so comically related her mother's intention of poisoning his wife, if one existed. Or even last night, when a lady in a red dress, a stolen bracelet in her slender hand, had gazed at him with panic in her eyes.

"Damn," he said softly.

"All this talk about honor," Skye murmured, "because you're a gambler, and her father lost her home in a poker game. So she asked you—or you're asking yourself—if there are any lines you won't cross. There are, Dane. You think I don't know after all these years?"

"How can you, when I don't?"

"But you do know. That certainty was always yours, or you'd have never gotten into this business. It's being in love—with her in particular—that's thrown you. You've already committed yourself to this job, which is one instance of integrity, by the way; you're stuck in the masquerade for the duration, and it's sheer habit to stick to those half-truths you were talking about. She's got buckets of doubts, understandable after what happened to her father. But I didn't notice those doubts holding her off very far a few minutes ago."

"Voyeur," Dane muttered, but with a spark of amusement.

Satisfied with the reaction, Skye went on calmly. "I'd be willing to bet, assuming Jennifer's instincts are in good working order, that she knows integrity when she sees it. She'll probably be mad as hell when you finally confess, but I doubt she'll be very much surprised."

"She could never love a gambler," Dane said roughly.

"She's already loved one," Skye pointed out, and before his partner could respond, he added, "And, to you, gambling is business. The odds and skill fascinate you, not the winning. You might have folded a few times with a winning hand, but you've never dealt off the bottom to win. That's another line you haven't crossed."

"I may have to cross it this time."

After a moment, Skye asked, "Is Kelly that good?"

"Rumor has it. And unless he starts passing that phony money from the start, I'll have to back him right to the wall. We don't have a hope in hell of finding that press unless he leads us to it, and I doubt he'll go anywhere near it until he needs money badly. I have to win this time. I have to."

"It's business, Dane."

"No. This time, it's personal. I *want* to beat him. Don't you see? I can't tell myself there's a precise line between right and wrong, a line I'm balancing on. Not this time."

"You want to beat him because you're in love with Jennifer. Hell, it's so obvious. *That* is your point of honor. You can't stomach what Kelly did to Jennifer and her mother; you can't walk away from it; and you can't leave somebody else to clean up the mess. You promised her she'd have her home back. And you'll get it back for her, come hell or high water. Because you love her, and you made a promise. If that isn't integrity, then I don't know what is."

Dane chuckled suddenly, the sound of balance restored. "I don't know if you're right, but it sounds good."

"I'm right. Trust me."

After a glance at the luminous dial of his watch, Dane murmured, "Ten minutes until dinner. God, this has been the longest hour of my life. They'll think I'm lost out here." He looked at his partner. "Why were you looking for me?"

"A slight hitch in the plan."

"You couldn't find Seton's room?"

"Oh, I found the room. And Seton found me in it, worse luck. The only thing I could think of was to have him pack a bag quick and get him out of there."

Dane frowned a little. "So Kelly will assume he got nervous when Jenny showed up, and bolted?"

"Cross your fingers."

"Where is he now?"

"He had an excuse for a car parked out back, so I trussed him up and put him in the backseat. There's a service road leading to the main highway; I drove a little way along it and pulled off. That's three ways onto this place I've counted," he added parenthetically. "Security must be hell."

Dane was thinking it through. "The plate?"

"Top shelf of his closet. Kelly should find it easily enough, I'd think."

"Okay. What'll we do with Seton?"

"I've considered that. Remember Tony from Baton Rouge?"

"Of course I remember."

"I'll give him a call. He owes us one, so he'll be happy to keep an eye on Seton until we can get the rest of this cleared up. Two hours by car, and he's here."

Dane nodded slowly. "Good enough."

"I thought so."

"You have any trouble with Seton?"

"Did he try to be a cowboy, you mean? No. He came along meek as a lamb."

Dane wasn't surprised. He'd seen hulking brutes who bashed people's heads in for fun obey Skye without a murmur. "All right, then. We go on from here as planned."

•   •   •

Dane met his host halfway back to the veranda, and Garrett Kelly's brows lifted at the sight of him.

"We were wondering about you," he said politely.

"I'm part cat," Dane told him in an easy, lazy tone. "Never happy until I've found all the corners. Lost track of time, I'm afraid."

"You should have worked up an appetite, then," Kelly said.

"Yes. Yes, I certainly have."

Five

Jennifer hardly knew how to respond to her mother's inevitable questions after she returned from Belle Retour and Dane. She was still trapped in that peculiar feeling of suspension, of waiting, poised without breath on the edge of something. But she had underestimated her mother. Francesca, after one penetrating look at Jennifer, merely smiled and asked nothing.

That reaction bothered Jennifer, and when she went to wash up before dinner she took the opportunity to look into a mirror, searching for whatever it was that her mother had seen. But she looked familiar to her own eyes, unchanged. A bit pale, perhaps, but that was nothing.

Surely that was nothing.

She slept fitfully that night, waking often with a start, her heart pounding. Morning brought her the grim awareness of her own scattered emotions, and she made a determined effort to gain control over herself. The result, and one she was all too aware of, was that she achieved a kind of surface calm, beneath which nothing changed.

She didn't want to think, and retreated to her study immediately after breakfast to work. Since she was a freelance commerical artist, she usually worked at home, and managed to immerse herself in her routine. For at least several hours, she kept her mind blank, trusting to automatic awareness of her work. But after lunch she couldn't recapture that mood, and sat at her board, a half-finished layout pinned before her.

Damn. She wondered who had triumphed in the test of poker skill last night between Dane and Kelly. She wondered if Kelly had let slip anything that might have told Dane the plate had been recovered. She wondered if she'd ever see Dane again.

The last was a haunting question. She had met him only the night before last, after all, and knew almost nothing about him . . . except that by his own admission he was a gambler and a thief. He was after something from Kelly, that much appeared obvious. But what? A counterfeit plate, he had said. But what proof did she have that such a thing even existed? She hadn't seen it.

Yes, Kelly had clearly been robbed of something—but had it been a plate? And she had only Dane's word that whatever the item was, it had been returned to Kelly.

The sheer force of his personality had carried her along, unsettled but obeying, doubting his explanations yet allowing him to half convince her he was telling the truth.

She realized suddenly, miserably, that he would make an excellent confidence man; he had the uncanny ability to inspire belief even in the face of doubt. And Jennifer couldn't help but wonder if he was playing on her emotions like a master manipulator, using her in some dark game of his own.

Her own response to him was easy to explain, she assured herself. She had been out of control for the first time in her adult life. That was why she had responded so wildly, why she had reacted with such abandon. It hadn't been *him*, it had been herself. She had been . . . oversensitive to everything, including his touch, his kisses. That was all. *All.*

"Jennifer! Those trousers—"

"Jeans. I'm working, Mother." She picked up a pencil, frowning, trying to look as though that was the truth.

"You have a visitor," Francesca said gently.

Jennifer felt her heart catch, but managed to keep her voice even. "Oh? I wasn't expecting anyone." And she hadn't heard the doorbell.

Her mother's laugh was throaty. "This one would always be unexpected, I think. So handsome! And such charm, ah, I knew he was your man!"

Wincing, Jennifer murmured, "Dane?"

"But of course. Such manners, that one. He asked me if he might take you out this afternoon. Naturally, I said that he had my blessing."

Jennifer slid off her stool, staring at her mother with increasing alarm. It didn't surprise her that Dane had won Francesca over so quickly; her mother was predisposed to love charming men with gallant manners, and Dane was undoubtedly that. "Mother, you didn't . . . you didn't say—"

Francesca lifted a scornful brow. "My baby, would

that be subtle? Of course, I did not say that I knew he was your man. This is for *him* to tell *me*. And he will." She nodded decisively. "But now, you must change."

"I will not," Jennifer said stubbornly. "And I'm not going anywhere with him." She drew a short breath. "He's a gambler, Mother. A *gambler*."

Francesca didn't look surprised, but only thoughtful. She studied her daughter for a moment, then shrugged carelessly. "Then you must tell him that, my baby."

Jennifer tossed her pencil aside and squared her shoulders. She turned away from her mother and left the room, unsurprised when Francesca didn't accompany her. Holding on to her fragile surface control, she went into the small living room, determined to stop this insanity. But when she halted two steps into the room and saw him, she couldn't seem to find the words.

He was standing by the fireplace, gazing up at a beautifully framed sketch done in pastels that hung above the mantel. The drawing was of Rufus Chantry, and he was, curiously, dressed as Dane was dressed now, in light-colored sports jacket and pants with a white shirt open at the throat.

"Yours?" Dane questioned softly without looking at her.

"Yes," she answered, admitting to being the artist.

He turned to face her, smiling a little but with unreadable eyes. "A characteristic pose, holding a deck of cards?"

Jennifer glanced past him at the sketch, and felt her throat tighten. "It was the only time he was still," she said, admitting nothing now.

Dane nodded. "I see. Your eyes are gray."

She looked back at him, caught off guard.

"The morning brought doubts, obviously," he murmured.

She wondered if her eyes really did change color, or if that was only his idea. "The doubts were already there," she said in an even tone. "I just took a long hard look at them."

"And condemned me without a trial?"

Jennifer felt something inside her turn over with a thud. Oh, he was good, she reminded herself fiercely. He was so good she could feel herself responding to him, even now. That beautiful voice of his controlled just a hint of sadness or bitterness; his smile was crooked, his eyes shadowed and unreadable. Her impulse was to blurt, *I'm sorry!* because something told her she had hurt him with her doubts, but she held the apology back.

"I don't know why you're here," she said, ignoring his question.

He came to her slowly, but made no effort to touch her when he stood before her. "Will you go for a drive with me?" he asked softly.

"I'm working." Tautly, she added, "Some other time."

"We need to talk, Jenny."

"I've taken myself out of the game," she told him.

"It isn't a game," he said, suddenly rough. "If it was, I wouldn't be here. I *shouldn't* be here, Jenny, because if Kelly found out—Look, I just want to spend some time with you. Will you come with me?"

She could feel herself weakening, feel the surface control melting away like a thin layer of ice heated from below. Against all reason, she wanted to be with him. "I don't trust you," she heard herself saying bitterly.

"I know." He took her hand and led her toward the front door, as if he knew she would go.

Jennifer didn't protest. She allowed him to take her out to his rented car, which was a gleaming white Ferrari, and put her into the passenger seat. She watched him move around the car and gracefully fit his big frame behind the wheel.

"Why do big men always drive sports cars?" she asked idly.

Dane sent her a faint smile as he started the powerful car and put it into gear. "Some macho thing, I suppose."

"Don't you know?" She was smiling despite herself.

"I've never thought about it." He guided the car out of the driveway and onto the main road, heading for Lake Charles. "Personally, I just like sports cars. They're powerful, maneuverable, fast." He sent her another glance, this one full of irony. "Sometimes, the answers are simple ones."

"And sometimes they aren't." She watched his hands on the wheel, beautiful and powerful, remembered them on her body, moving her unbearably. She tried to block those images and sensations, tried to ignore them. It hadn't been *Dane*, she reminded herself grimly; it had been she. Her lack of control. Her emotions spilling over. "Did you win last night?"

"No."

"Was that intentional?"

He shrugged slightly. "I wasn't trying too hard, if that's what you mean. I was sizing him up, studying him."

"He won?"

Dane nodded. "He came out ahead."

"Did he cheat?"

After a moment, Dane said, "When I told you that I know how to spot someone else cheating, I meant that. It's part of my reputation as a gambler. I made sure Kelly knew it. He doesn't need to cheat, Jenny. He's good."

She half turned in her seat, looking at him. "Better than you?" she asked.

"I don't know. Maybe. I'll find out tonight."

Jennifer was trying to concentrate on what they were saying, fighting to ignore her body's response to his nearness. Only the gear console separated them, and she was all too conscious of his big, powerful body so close. But it was just a memory; she didn't really *feel* anything, she thought. "Do you have to beat him? I mean, is that part of the plan?"

Dane frowned. "Kelly's had some business losses the past year or so. He's close to bankruptcy. Like most gamblers, he believes he can win enough to straighten out his finances. He's also smart enough to know that it wouldn't be wise to try and win that much from his usual poker cronies; he got into the neighborhood that way, but if he kept beating them . . ."

"No one would want to play against him?"

"Exactly."

"Which is why you're here," she guessed.

Nodding, Dane said, "An old friend of Kelly's is a high stakes poker player, world-class. Kelly called him and more or less asked him to find another gambler with money to lose. He called me; we've played against each other down in Miami. I came out here with him, and to that party night before last, specifically to be introduced and invited to play poker with Garrett Kelly and his group."

"Isn't that unusual?" she asked. "To come all this way?"

"No. My reputation is that I'll go anywhere for a good game. There are about a dozen of us like that, scattered around the country."

"With money to lose."

Dane glanced at her again, hearing the note in her voice that resonated with bitterness. Then he looked ahead, concentrated on driving, and when he spoke, he kept his voice deliberate. "Kelly's friend called me last week; I was busy at the time. Then I called him back and told him I was interested."

"Because of the friend who wanted you to check Kelly's safe?" she asked, trying to keep her voice even.

"Yes. She'd already found out Kelly was a high-stakes player, and thought I could get in there easier than anyone else she knew. It was a good idea, and it worked."

She? The brunette, Jennifer thought, but didn't ask. "And then you found the plate."

"Unexpectedly, yes."

Jennifer was silent for a few moments, working through the information. "So your plan now is to strain Kelly's resources so that he has to print counterfeit money?"

"He didn't pass any last night, but he doesn't have much cash on hand; he keeps it in that safe. If I can push him right to the wall, make him bet all the cash he has and then win it from him, he'll have to do something."

"He could be printing the money now."

Dane hesitated, then said, "If so, we'll know where

the press is hidden. I have a partner working with me, Jenny. He's watching Belle Retour. One of us will have Kelly under observation constantly."

Jennifer stared at him, baffled. "Dane, none of this makes sense."

"Doesn't it?"

She felt tense, uncertain. "No. It's—it's out of character for a gambler to be doing what you're doing. Even a professional gambler. If what you've told me is the truth, then you have to be something more. Something else."

He was silent for a few moments, then swore under his breath and turned the car off the main road near a park, finally stopping it and turning the engine off. In the distance, they could see the Calcasieu River.

Dane half turned toward her. "Jenny, I want you to understand something. I'm a gambler. By nature, by inclination, and by profession. I've won and lost more than one fortune. This week I could stake two houses, a condo, and a yacht—in a week, I may well be the next best thing to broke. That's a *fact,* and nothing else can change it. Believe that. It's the truth."

"But there's more," she said, powerfully feeling the truth of her words.

He sighed roughly. "There's always more. Over the years, I've made a number of friends in the intelligence community. It's not so surprising; I'm often in a position to know things, to be aware of—well, movements and such. So I became an information broker. You might say it's a fringe benefit of being a world-class poker player. And sometimes, when an agent asks me to cultivate a certain person, to try to get a particular piece of information, I do."

"This friend of yours, she's an agent?"

"She was. Retired now, and happily married. Her husband is a very powerful man, and someone's trying to get at him. The trail led to Kelly."

Jennifer drew a deep breath. "And your partner? He's an agent, isn't he?"

"Yes. And my best friend." Dane smiled a bit crookedly. "I haven't explained this much to anyone in ten years. I can't prove any of it, Jenny."

She nodded slowly. "I know. But I believe you."

"Why?" he asked curiously. "It all sounds so unlikely. Intelligence agents, counterfeit operations, powerful men with secret enemies—and me, a gambler, the pivot."

"Maybe that's why I believe it." She smiled faintly. "Because it sounds so unlikely. It's too elaborate to be a lie. Too involved."

"Does that mean you trust me now?"

"I trust what you're doing. It makes sense; it explains why you're here."

"But you still don't trust me."

Jennifer hesitated, still refusing to believe what her instincts and intuition insisted she believe: that she could trust him with every part of herself, even her heart. It was absurd, irrational, just the residue of powerful emotions freed by her own lack of control. "I don't know," she heard herself say finally. "You've told me *what* you are, but not *who* you are. I still don't have that answer."

"Not one of the simple answers, I guess." He turned his gaze toward the windshield, frowning again. "You always think you know who you are. Until someone asks. Then all you can answer with are a few concrete facts. Want to hear those?"

"Yes." She was watching his profile, listening to his deep, beautiful voice.

"All right. I'm thirty-five, born in Chicago and raised there. My parents still live there. I have a sister and brother, both younger. And I worked my way through college by waiting tables and playing poker."

"Do you have a degree?" she asked curiously.

He looked at her with a sudden smile. "Yes. Law." His voice was dry, fully appreciative of the irony.

Jennifer had to smile. "You were never tempted to practice?"

"Not really. There are already too many lawyers in the world."

"And a welcome dearth of gamblers?"

"*Skilled* gamblers, yes."

"So you just became one?"

Dane was silent for a moment, then said slowly, "I won a fortune. I'd been trying to decide if I wanted to practice law. What I wanted to do with the rest of my life. Then I got involved in a high-stakes game. A friend with a lot more money than I had staked me. He said he'd put up the money, and I'd keep half the winnings if there were any. He believed I could win, and I did. Half the winnings turned out to be a fortune. I never looked back."

She gazed at him, conscious of some emotion she couldn't quite put her finger on. What was it? The feeling that there was more to this, that Dane was holding back some vital bit of information. It was something elusive, and she couldn't grasp it. "No roots?" she asked.

"I carry my roots around with me." He smiled faintly. "No regrets, Jenny."

"Have you ever lost everything?"

"Everything I bet, yes. Everything I had, no. That's the professional part of me. If I lost everything, I'd have nothing to rebuild with."

"That's the way you think of it? Rebuilding?"

"Sure."

They were silent for a while, Jennifer gazing out through the windshield and Dane watching her. Then, quietly, he asked, "Are we going to talk about us now?"

She refused to look at him. Her surface control was fragile at best, and she was afraid of what lay underneath it. There was too much that was instinctive and wild. And not real. Her feelings couldn't be real. Wary of where they might take her, she didn't trust the feelings. She'd make a fool of herself again, imagining—

"Jenny?"

"Why me?" she asked, still not looking at him. "It was very sudden. Or do you have a girl along with a poker game in every city?"

Dane looked at her face, lovely and serious, then at the slender hands laced tightly together in her lap. The glossy shell of calm she wore was just that, he knew. What he didn't know was how she really felt about him. Mistrustful, certainly. He could make her want him, but he was too experienced not to know that desire could exist without deeper feelings. He thought she was cautious now, still surprised and unsettled by her emotional storm of yesterday, and had probably begun doubting her own feelings, her response to him.

And he was a gambler, everything she most mistrusted.

He waited until she looked at him, then said, "I didn't plan on you. I shouldn't even be with you, Jenny.

But I couldn't stay away." He hesitated, then added harshly, "I know I'm the last man in the world you want to get involved with. I guess you didn't plan on me either."

"No, I didn't." Caught again by his eyes, she couldn't look away. "I don't know what you want from me."

Dane reached out slowly and smoothed a strand of pale gold away from her cheek. She wore her hair loosely today, falling over her shoulders like silk, and his hand slid around to the soft nape of her neck, under the warm weight of it. He could feel her tremble, and his own body tensed in an instant response.

"What can I say to that?" he murmured.

"The truth." Her voice was husky, almost a plea.

Dane hesitated, but he didn't dare tell her how he felt. Not yet—if he ever could. It might turn out to be something she would never want to hear from him. "I want a chance. That's all, Jenny. We both know there's something between us. All I want is a chance to find out what it is."

It wasn't *real*, Jennifer thought wildly, feeling herself drawn slowly toward him. Those feelings of yesterday . . . But they were rising inside her again, with nothing but him to trigger them, no previous outburst to blast her control into splinters.

When his lips touched hers she wanted to hold herself stiffly, but it was impossible. The console separated them below the waist, and Dane made no effort to pull her upper body against his. His right hand remained curled around her neck, and his left hand rested gently over both hers. He kissed her without force, a slow, gradually deepening seduction.

Jennifer couldn't fight the sensations—or him. And

she couldn't deny, this time, that he ignited the feelings inside her.

The slow probing of his tongue, a secret caress, filled her senses with building heat, and she was swaying toward him without thought. She wanted him, as quickly as that, as certain as she had been before. She wanted him, and didn't care where they were or what tomorrow would bring.

A rough sound escaped Dane when his lips left hers, and both his hands cupped her face warmly. "You see?" he murmured huskily. "Neither of us can ignore this, Jenny."

She stared into darkly purple eyes, got lost in them, and made the only denial left to her. "It's just chemistry," she whispered. "I can't feel anything more than that. Not for you!" She wanted to recall the words immediately, but it was too late.

His face paled, and Dane released her instantly, drawing away from her both physically and emotionally. He sat gazing through the windshield for a moment, then silently started the car and turned them back toward her house.

"You're a gambler," she said softly, her entire body aching, emotions in turmoil.

"I understand. It's all right, Jenny." His voice was very quiet and steady. "I knew the odds were against me."

Jennifer couldn't take her eyes off his face, some part of her shocked to see that it meant so much to him. And some part of her was bleeding, because she had cut herself with the same knife she had used to cut him. "I can't help it," she said, because she had to say something.

"I know. Neither of us can help being what we are." He smiled faintly, and said with a lightness that didn't hide the hurt beneath it, "I should have become a lawyer."

She was losing something and knew it, and the pain of that loss was worse than anything she'd felt before. But the trauma of her father's gambling had affected her too deeply to be easily set aside, and she knew that too.

After a moment of silence, Dane said, still with deceptive lightness, "I think I knew there was no chance when I saw your sketch of your father. There's a lot of love in the picture. And a great deal of bitterness. Was it a deliberate choice, the cards fanned out on the table in front of him?"

"Yes," she answered softly.

Dane nodded. "I thought so. A possible royal flush, in spades, with one card facedown."

She sat very still, watching him, afraid that if she moved at all, she'd shatter. The tension between them was something stark and alive, contained only by this unnatural, deceptive calm they both wore like shields. It was visible in the whiteness of his hands as they gripped the steering wheel, in her own tightly laced fingers lying so still in her lap. They were both conscious of it, both holding it at bay with quiet words and motionless bodies, as if to release it meant something terrible.

Jennifer felt her whole body resist the volition of her mind, felt her breathing grow more ragged, her heart pound even harder. All her senses cried out to ignore reason and give in to the more simple reality of need and desire. She refused to love him, but she needed him, wanted him, and her body insisted that was enough for now. She would never have believed that she could want a man with such blind intensity even while knowing—*knowing*—that the next step forward might bring only pain.

"Tell me gambling doesn't matter to you," she whispered suddenly, unable to stop the words. "Tell me you can give it up without hesitation."

"I can't." His voice was bleak. "I won't lie to you about that, Jenny. I am what I am."

"And you won't change?"

He hesitated. "It's too late for me to change. I want to promise I'd never hurt you the way your father did, but what's that promise worth when you don't trust me?"

"I want to trust you. But . . ."

Dane nodded jerkily, as if his own control was dissolving. "I know. You can't trust me because I'm a gambler, and I can't be anything else."

"It hurt so much, what Dad did to us," she said unsteadily, trying to explain what he already seemed to understand. "My whole life changed. Belle Retour was more than just home, and when he lost it so damned easily and quickly, it seemed as if . . . as if nothing could be forever. As if there was no certainty left. One turn of a card, and all my roots were cut away from me." She caught her breath, trying not to cry out with the pain she felt. "I can't risk that happening again. I'd never survive it again!"

Jennifer hadn't realized she felt that way; it was something she had hidden from herself. But he had drawn it out of her, just as he had drawn out so much else. And he was even more pale now, his white face more still, as if every heartfelt word she had thrown at him had been a knife.

"All right," he said softly. "All right, Jenny."

She tried to gain control of herself, to breathe deeply, but she couldn't. She was only vaguely aware that they had reached her house, that he had stopped the car in the driveway. He got out and came around to open her door, and she moved automatically to step out onto the drive.

But when he closed the door and took a step back away from her, her frail control broke, and she couldn't just let him go. Her arms went around his waist and she pressed her face against his chest, holding on to him.

Dane's body was rigid, his heart pounding heavily, but his arms were gentle when they slipped around her.

"Damn you," she whispered raggedly.

He hugged her briefly, an almost convulsive movement of strength and possession, then gently forced her arms away and stepped back from her. His smile was only a ghost of the charming, crooked one he usually wore. "I'll come back when it's all over, and tell you about it," he said in that light voice that wasn't. "When we finally get Kelly."

She nodded, unable to say another word, and turned away from him stiffly, aching. And she didn't look back as she walked to the front door. She opened it and went inside, closing it behind her and leaning back against it. She heard the Ferrari roar away, the first hint of violence from Dane implicit in the uncontrolled sound.

"Jennifer?"

She looked up as Francesca approached her, watched her mother's face go still in a sudden awareness.

"My baby . . ."

Jennifer heard a soft laugh escape her throat in a sound that held no humor. "What am I going to do, Mama?" she murmured. "What am I going to do now?"

It was sheer luck Dane didn't get stopped by the highway patrol on his way back to the hotel. He handled the car with an expert driver's automatic awareness, but made no effort to leash the Ferrari's powerful engine. More than one speed limit sign quivered in the wake of his passing, and more than one other driver felt his own vehicle lean toward the shoulder of the road as if cringing away from the low-slung white fury rocketing by.

Dane slowed the car at last when he reached the hotel. Moments later, he was up in his suite with no memory of having parked the car or walked through the lobby. He paced without thought, and when the phone rang minutes or hours later, he picked it up and answered automatically.

"Hello?"

"Dane, it's Raven." Her innately cheerful voice was brisk. "Have you got anything yet?"

He pondered the question for a moment, until the submerged, professional part of him fought its way to the surface of his numb mind. "Something," he said without inflection, remembering what Skye had found out last night from Brady Seton. "But it may be only half the story. I'd rather not explain until I know for sure. A few days, I think."

There was a pause, and then Raven said, "Are you all right? You sound . . . very tired."

"I'll be all right," he said, and wondered how long it would be before that statement became true. If it ever did. "Kelly's a night owl; he likes to play until dawn."

"If you say so." She didn't really sound convinced. "I wanted to remind you, if you need more money—"

"No. I can't use your money now, Raven. I'll wire it back first thing in the morning."

"What? Dane, this whole thing was my idea, my problem. You can't bet your own money when you're helping me!"

He drew a deep breath and let it out slowly. "It's more than that now. It became personal to me. I have my reasons, and I'll tell you about them later. In the meantime, just accept that I have to beat Garrett Kelly with my own money."

"What if you lose?" she asked soberly.

"I won't. This time, winning's too important."

She was silent for a long moment, then sighed. "I hope you know what you're doing, pal."

"I know. I'll be in touch within a few days, Raven."

"All right. Good luck."

"Thanks."

He cradled the receiver and stood gazing at nothing. He knew what he was doing. He was keeping a promise. No matter what happened or what it cost him, Jennifer would have her Belle Retour back when it was over.

Six

The clock on the mantel ticked steadily on in the quiet of the room. The only light came from a lamp suspended low over a round table near the window. Cigarette and cigar smoke rose upward to disappear into darkness, each tendril following the eddies and currents always present in even the most still room and caused now by air-conditioning and the breathing of the five men seated in comfortable chairs, cards in their hands or stacked neatly or flung down haphazardly on the green baize of the game table.

For serious gamblers such as these, poker chips remained in a caddy and out of the way: the rule was cash on the table. Stack of bills, arranged according to individual habit, lay before each man, and in the center of the table was a careless heap of money, all hundred-dollar bills.

The current pot was somewhere in the neighborhood of fifty thousand dollars.

Three men had folded, and they sat back, smoking or sipping their drinks, watching silently as the remaining two played the hand out. It was a game of bluff now, and had been for more than an hour, each man steadily raising the stakes in an effort to make the other lose his nerve and fold. Neither of them had requested a new card since it had become a duel. In fact, Dane's cards were stacked facedown near his relaxed hands, and he hadn't so much as looked at them in almost half an hour. Each time Garrett Kelly tossed a stack of bills into the pot, Dane simply matched, then raised the bet.

And it became increasingly difficult for Kelly to duplicate Dane's relaxed, almost indifferent air. He toyed with his cards, putting them down and picking them up a dozen times. He lit cigarette after cigarette. His peculiarly colorless eyes probed sharply across the table as he sought to find a hint of strain in that tranquil, handsome face, some sign of hesitation or uncertainty in the vivid eyes.

He found no crack in Dane's composure, and by this fourth night of playing against him, no man at the table was surprised by it. At least two of the men had gulped silently upon discovering that Dane never raised the bet in increments of less than five hundred dollars, but they were wealthy men and experienced gamblers, and had adjusted. What they continued to find incredible was Dane's utter stillness.

He appeared boneless in his chair, requiring neither cigarette nor drink as a prop, and having no apparent need to change position to ease the strain of sitting for so long. At the beginning of the hand, when there was much more activity around the table, his deep, charming voice had been heard as often as the other men's, but once the play had come down to only two, he had fallen silent. And as Kelly's tension increased, Dane seemed to become even more unruffled. His brilliant eyes appeared as serene as twin violet lakes, his lips remained curved in a crooked half smile; and his graceful hands moved only to flick more money into the pot.

It was just after midnight, and they had been playing since eight.

Kelly, still with a respectable pile of money before him, matched Dane's last bid of four thousand dollars, and was about to raise by another thousand when his opponent's lifted hand stopped him.

"Before you decide to raise," Dane said lazily, "maybe you'd better look at this." With his right hand only, he turned his top card faceup on the table. It was the ace of diamonds. Slowly, he turned the next three cards up. In a neat row before him lay a very possible royal flush in diamonds, ace, king, queen, jack. The fifth card remained facedown, and Dane tapped it lightly with an index finger.

"If this is a ten of diamonds," he said, still lazy, "you can't possibly beat me. There are no wild cards in the game, so you can't have five of a kind. And although it may be remotely possible that you're holding a royal flush yourself, it would be a first for me in twenty years. So you'd better decide if my hole card is a ten of diamonds."

The other three men leaned forward, their eyes moving from Dane's imperturbable face to Kelly's strained one. This, they all felt, was poker at its best, a game of strategy. Was Dane bluffing in a carefully calculated show of confidence, his hole card worthless, or did he indeed hold a hand Kelly wouldn't be able to beat?

A long moment passed, and then Kelly nodded jerkily at the bid he had already placed into the pot. "Call."

Smiling faintly, Dane tossed another ten thousand into the pot. "Raise," he said.

Kelly hesitated, but then his nerve broke. Swearing, he slapped his cards facedown. "I'm out," he said heavily. Then, as if he couldn't help himself, he said, "Were you bluffing?"

Dane didn't have to answer that, but he quite deliberately flipped over his hole card. It was a three of diamonds.

Kelly closed his eyes briefly, then reached for the hand he'd abandoned and showed it to the others. He had been holding a straight, king high, in hearts and clubs. He would have won if he had called Dane's bluff.

The tension in the room eased, and a murmur of discussion broke out. While Dane was collecting his winnings, as tranquil as he'd been all along, Kelly glanced at his watch and then rose.

"I think we could all use a break, gentlemen. Stretch your legs if you like, while I get some sandwiches for us." A bit stiff from having sat for so long, he walked slowly from the room.

The other men rose as well, stretching and wandering around. Someone turned on a few other lamps, so that the room looked more like a parlor and less like a gambling den. They left cards and money on the table, just as Dane did when he rose with his usual grace and strolled casually out of the room.

"He's not human," one of the men muttered to another.

Out in the hallway, Dane grimaced faintly as he heard the comment, but didn't pause or turn around. And it wasn't until he reached the portrait gallery that he flexed his shoulders to ease the ache between them. Wandering down the long hallway, he looked absently at the paintings. The only illumination in the corridor came from the portraits' individual lights, which were always on at night. Dane had made it obvious that the paintings fascinated him, to the point that Kelly was no longer surprised to find him wandering along the corridor at odd times staring intently at the portraits.

The real reason Dane came here was that it was a central location in the house, and a perfect place to make contact with Skye. This was the most dangerous time for them, both inside the house, with Kelly's remaining security man roaming about. Dane wasn't even sure Skye would be here yet. He had planned to use at least the first few hours of the poker games for sleep, while Dane could watch their quarry.

But Dane wasn't surprised to hear his partner's low voice just as he reached the end of the hallway, because Skye required little sleep, especially when they were working.

"Kelly still hasn't replaced Seton; has he mentioned his lost security guard?"

"Interestingly, yes," Dane replied in an identical soft tone that couldn't have been heard from three feet away. "One of the other men commented that there seemed to be one less security man. Kelly said something about it being unwise to hire relatives."

"Relatives? Damn, we missed that."

"Something else. Kelly's openly scornful that his relative flunked out with quote, some federal outfit up north, end quote. So when Seton told you he was carrying a badge during his clumsy feint at Josh Long, he may well have been telling the truth."

After a moment, Skye said, "Hagen."

"That's my bet. We'll find out for sure once we have Kelly wrapped up nicely."

"Let me be the one to tell Raven if that's the case," Skye requested. He sighed. "We should be about ready to wind down on this. You could have taken him with that hand," he said, having obviously been close enough to the parlor earlier to hear what had transpired there. "He would have kept raising."

"Probably," Dane agreed in a murmur, standing where he was and gazing at the portrait hanging before him. Skye was to his left, completely hidden in the darkness of a doorway. "But we haven't found the press yet, and he hasn't passed any phony money. I don't want to panic him with just one hand."

"He has to be feeling the strain," Skye observed thoughtfully. "How much have you hit him for so far tonight?"

"Fifty thousand, more or less. He had close to a hundred in his safe the other night. The way it stands since that last hand, he's lost two thirds of what he started out with."

There was a short silence, and then Skye said, "We won't find the press in the house, you know that. I've already checked nearly every room. You're going to have to win all the cash he's got, and force him to lead us to it."

"Yes. I know."

"What's on your mind?" Skye asked perceptively.

After a moment, Dane answered, "Tomorrow night's

game—if I manage to win it all tonight. Kelly's sure to want another shot at me."

"So?"

"I did some figuring this afternoon. If our information on Kelly is accurate, his only assets are this plantation and house. The plantation is the biggest in this part of the state, more than three hundred acres, mostly rice and timber. It's in the red at the moment because he's borrowed heavily against it and the income just barely covers the mortgage. Even so, the market value is easily into seven figures, and he could expect to stake close to a million with it discounting the mortgage. The house is crammed with two hundred years of history, most of it valuable, so add another million at the very least."

Quietly, Skye said, "Your promise to Jennifer."

Dane nodded, still gazing at the portrait of a proudly erect Chantry in the uniform of a Confederate soldier. "I can match Kelly's assets unless he goes berserk and prints a few hundred thousand worthless dollars. In that case, I'll have to accept them at face value, and even if I win every dollar on the table tonight, I may not have enough to force him to stake Belle Retour."

Skye sighed. "Then, somehow, we've got to prevent Kelly from printing any more than a hundred grand *without* alerting him that we're on to him. You're better with machines than I am; when we find the damned thing, you'll have to cripple it—slightly."

"And so carefully that he won't know it was tampered with? Damn. I'd better make some calls tomorrow. I don't suppose you know anyone who knows how to gently disable a counterfeit press?"

"Not offhand, no."

Dane said something a great deal stronger than "damn."

"It's your own fault," Skye reminded him dryly. "You *will* keep on making promises." With no change in tone, he added, "Speaking of which, how's Jennifer? You haven't mentioned her the last couple of days. Have you even seen her?"

Dane had hoped to avoid that subject with Skye; though the men he played poker against might well believe his composure was nearly inhuman, his partner knew only too well there was a very normal, feeling man beneath the tranquil mask. But Dane had to answer, because in their life, the truth was all too often possible *only* between the two of them.

"No. She's wise enough not to get burned twice," he said finally, steadily.

"Are you both so sure she would be burned?" Skye didn't sound surprised, as if he'd expected this.

"She isn't willing to risk it. I can't blame her for that." Dane shifted restlessly. "I have to get back, or Kelly will come looking for me."

"Wait." Skye was silent for a moment, and when he spoke his voice was unusually sober. "If you walk away from her, you'll never be the same. Neither will she."

"What she feels about her father's betrayal runs deep. I don't know how to fight it . . . or even if I can."

"You'd never hurt her the way he did."

"How do I convince her of that?"

"Any way you can. As long as you *do*." Skye's low voice, curiously disembodied because he was hidden in darkness, might have been the voice Dane had been trying to ignore since he had left Jennifer at her house days ago. The voice urging him to *try*, to keep trying until he somehow found a way through the wall between them. He had tried to ignore the voice because he knew what he would risk in the attempt, and the gambler in him was wary, mistrustful of the odds against winning.

He would have to risk everything. Not the way he would willingly risk material things to keep his promise to Jennifer, but a different, far more painful risk. Himself. Everything he was, his weaknesses as well as his strengths, his self-doubts and inner torments along with his certainties and convictions. With her own wounds, Jennifer would never trust and believe in him until she saw him clearly.

Loving her, Dane was willing to bare himself to her, but after so many years of too many gambles, he was half afraid she would see nothing worthy of trust or belief when he found a way to shine a light on all the dark places in his soul. And that would be no surface rejection, mistrusting him because he was a gambler, because of what he *did*. That would be a rejection of what he *was*, of the very foundation of him—and it would be one he'd never survive.

"I have to go," he told his partner quietly. Then, just before he turned away, he added, "I hope you brought along some coffee; you may have a long watch after I leave him the morning."

"No problem," Skye murmured.

Dane strolled back up the hall toward the parlor, mentally pulling on his mask—and finding it less of a mask now. There was, he realized, something to be said for accepting what had to be, even if it was potentially painful.

Risk hell to win heaven. He thought that now, finally, he was willing to risk everything.

It was past four A.M. and the men in the parlor had discarded their jackets and loosened their ties. In the last three hands, Dane had folded early, yet the majority of the money on the table still lay before him. Kelly's luck had been in and out; he had won the last hand with a skillful bluff, but had been forced to run the stakes far too high in order to do so.

Dane had been unobtrusively watching the other man, waiting for certain signs, and he saw them now. Kelly was clearly feeling the strain and yet, like so many gamblers, he continued to grow more intent, almost feverishly certain that the next hand would be the best. Dane knew that the other men hardly noticed their host's increasing desperation because the signs were almost imperceptible, but after twenty years of card playing Dane saw them clearly.

It was time to make his move, and Dane made it with the sure skill and total concentration of a professional. He took the next two hands in rapid succession, deliberately winning with colossal bluffs and making certain every man at the table realized it. By the third hand, after winning with a pair of threes that any one of the others at the table could have beaten, he had them caught in blind determination, and he knew it.

Kelly dealt, and Dane watched very carefully to make certain the other man used no tricks. If he had, Dane's only choice would have been to fold instantly rather than risk losing. But there were no tricks, and Dane found himself holding three kings, an ace, and a deuce;

since the dealer's choice had made aces wild in this game, it meant he had four of a kind. He discarded the deuce, and in its place, Lady Luck smiling brilliantly down on him, was dealt another ace. He had five of a kind now, kings. The winning hand.

It was far better than he had hoped for, and his only task was to continue raising the stakes until he forced Kelly to bet all the cash he had. He knew the older man was blindly bent on recovering his losses, just as the other men were, all caught in the gambler's compulsive drive to win.

There was a round of discards and newly dealt cards, and then all settled down with the hands they had decided to play. At first singly and then in increasing numbers, hundred-dollar bills fluttered to the center of the table.

"I'm out," one man grunted, tossing his cards down because he had nothing left on the table to bet.

Ten minutes later, a second man folded. It had come down to three players.

"Call. Raise three hundred."

"Call. Two hundred up."

"Call. Another five."

"Damn. I'm out."

Two players now, Dane and Kelly. Dane watched the other man calmly as they played, vaguely curious, as always, to observe the signs of desperation, of recklessness. He had seen it before, often, but had never felt it himself. Satisfied when he beat the odds, mildly annoyed when he didn't, Dane had always considered poker just a game. He had more than once bet most of what he had, but material possessions had never meant a great deal to him, so in that sense he never bet more than he could afford to lose.

As Skye had observed, Dane enjoyed the game for its own sake, and though he had perfected the composure and skill of a professional gambler, he could shrug off winning as easily as losing with little involvement of his emotions. That was his professional edge.

He watched Kelly now, knowing the older man had a good hand simply by the excited glitter in his eyes. But knowing that his own hand couldn't be beaten gave Dane the leisure not to worry about strategy or tactics; all he had to do was keep raising the stakes. And since Dane never changed expression, nor gave himself away with a single movement or mannerism no matter what kind of hand he held, Kelly had no way of knowing that he had already lost every cent on the table.

The clock on the mantel ticked loudly in the tense silence while the pile of money grew steadily higher.

"Half a million on the table," one of the other men murmured in a kind of fascination, having obviously kept a running tally of the money bet.

Dane glanced at him, then returned his gaze to the cards he was holding. He had measured Kelly's remaining stake, and knew his opponent had twenty thousand left to bet; as for himself, he had fifty thousand in cash, and a cashier's check in his pocket for another hundred thousand. He was wondering now how far Kelly was willing to go tonight. But the only answer to that would be to find out.

He stacked his cards facedown, saying pleasantly, "It's almost dawn; why don't we finish this up for the night?" He drew the cashier's check from his jacket pocket and placed it, along with the fifty thousand in cash, into the pot. "Your last raise of ten thousand . . . and another hundred and forty thousand."

One of the other men grunted in surprise—or perhaps in awe—but that was the only sound.

Kelly's gaze was fixed on the mound of bills for a long moment, then lifted to Dane's steady, unreadable eyes. "I can't cover that in cash," he said, his voice strained. "Not with what I have on hand."

Dane shrugged slightly, and gave him the accepted gambler's answer, one they all understood very well. "Then you'd better fold."

Kelly looked at the hand he was holding, then shook his head. "I can have it by tomorrow night," he said in an attempt at casual certainty. "Get it from my bank later today."

That was a bald-faced lie, and Dane knew it. At best, Kelly had a few thousand left in his bank account. What he did apparently have, however, were the means to print his own money. But Dane had no intention of letting on he knew that. He shrugged again. "I'll take your I.O.U. in that case," he said calmly.

Two minutes later, a scrap of paper with Garrett Kelly's promise to pay one hundred twenty thousand dollars lay, along with his last twenty thousand in cash, in a pot that now totaled over three quarters of a million dollars.

"Call," Kelly said hoarsely.

Dane picked his cards up, fanned them out, and lay them faceup on the table. Kelly stared as if he couldn't believe it, while his unsteady fingers put his own cards on the table. He had a royal flush, in spades. Ironically enough, he had used a wild ace in place of the ace of spades—because that had been one of Dane's wild cards.

The sky was gray in the east as the men left the house, talking casually, men who could lose tens of thousands of dollars each and not mind very much. Except for one of them.

Kelly walked Dane out to his car, and he was composed in the way very desperate men can sometimes be, especially if they're gamblers with an irrational belief in luck. He was even smiling as Dane opened the door of his Ferrari and prepared to get in.

"I know we hadn't planned a game for tonight," he told Dane, "but how about it? Just you and me. It'll give me the chance to get even."

"Fine with me," Dane told him casually. "It'll have to be the final game, though, win, lose, or draw. I have to be getting back to Miami."

Kelly nodded agreeably. "Same time, then?"

"I'll be here." He got in and started the car, then followed the long, dark lane away from Belle Retour.

Jennifer thought of risks. Each night, restless in her bed, she thought. And felt. Sometimes during those long, lonely hours, she finally faced the inescapable fact that what she was feeling, what tormented her almost beyond bearing, was only partly caused by physical desire for a heartbreakingly handsome and charming man. Her body, she acknowledged with both relief and pain, had not become a separate entity apart from her mind and heart, beyond her control.

It was only that her body, free of the restraints of reason and bitter memories that held her mind and heart, had responded instantly to a truth too primitive to be denied. And now, alone in the dark, she faced that truth fully.

She was falling in love with Dane Prescott.

And it hurt. She wondered dimly if she would have felt with such depth and power if he had been a different kind of man, and knew somehow that she wouldn't have. An irony of life, perhaps, or of fate that she, with all her mistrust and bitterness toward gamblers, would fall helplessly in love with one.

Her mother knew from long experience of her daughter that Jennifer would resist interference; she was bound by her own nature to fight her way through her emotions alone. But she talked to her quietly when Jennifer had returned from her afternoon with Dane so shaken she could hardly think.

Francesca, with her acute perception of emotions, didn't hesitate to pinpoint the root of her daughter's confusion. "My baby . . . you must obey the greatest rule of life. *Do not anticipate pain.* It is a part of life, and of love. But if you wait for it, fearful and nervous, then you blind your heart to the joy of love."

"What if it happened again?" Jennifer had asked. "Dane's a gambler, he—"

"Do you love this man?"

"I–I think so. I didn't want to, but—"

Intensely, Francesca said, "Trust your love. And trust *him.* You must trust, Jennifer, or your doubt will destroy you both."

Struggling to lay those last doubts to rest, Jennifer finally asked her mother a question she had longed to ask for years. "What about you, Mother? How can you still feel like that after what Dad did to us?"

Francesca smiled gently. "We had twenty years together, my baby. He loved me, and he made me happy. Should I stop loving him now, or stop believing in love, because the ending was a painful one? *No.*"

"He lost your home," Jennifer whispered.

"He lost himself. Rufus was sick, Jennifer. I do not believe that your man has that sickness. But I do not know. Nor do you. Just as you do not know how many happy years lay ahead of you. There is little certainty in life, so there must be certainty in love. Give all your heart to this man—or give none of it. Anything less will only hurt you both."

Jennifer thought about that as the days passed. But her emotions were jumbled and uncertain. Still, she had to reach some kind of understanding, some peace with herself. She was falling in love with the last man she should have, and that was something she had to face and deal with.

But the days passed.

He probably has left anyway, she reflected tiredly as she showered and dressed. It was barely after eight in the morning, and she had met Dane less than a week before; she hadn't seen him in days. Now, in the silence of the house, her mother sleeping, Jennifer went to turn on the automatic coffee maker and then to get the morning paper.

The white Ferrari was parked in the driveway.

She didn't notice it until she straightened from picking up the newspaper, and by then Dane had gotten out and was coming toward her. She stood perfectly still, holding the rolled-up paper with both hands, strongly aware of a suddenly racing heart.

"I didn't know if you'd be up yet," he said quietly when he reached her.

Jennifer felt hungry, starving, and she couldn't stop looking at him. Odd, she had forgotten how incredibly handsome he was, but those eyes, like none she'd ever seen before . . . those eyes she remembered so well. "I'm an early riser," she managed to say. "You are too, I guess."

He shook his head slightly. "Not really. I usually have more late nights than early mornings. The game just broke up a few hours ago."

So that's why he's here. "It's over, then?" she asked.

He knew what she was asking. "No. Not quite. One more game tonight, and it will be. But I wanted to see you. Will you come have breakfast with me?"

Jennifer hesitated, fighting herself. "That wouldn't be very wise, would it?"

Dane smiled crookedly. "No."

Tomorrow, she thought, he'd be gone. "All—all right. Let me leave a note for my mother."

Five minutes later, she found herself back in the gleaming white sports car and heading for Lake Charles. Unwilling to let a silence grow between them, she ventured, "Aren't you tired?"

He shrugged. "No, I'm used to late nights. I'll catch a few hours' sleep later today."

Catch, she thought vaguely. Something on the run, something elusive. It bothered her. And he *was* tired, she realized, despite his words. There were no obvious physical signs, but she could sense something finely honed in him, as if some surface protection had been worn away by strain.

After a moment, she said, "Who won last night?"

"I did." He was matter-of-fact about it.

"Did Kelly cheat?"

Dane was silent for a moment, then shook his head. "No. And he lost a great deal last night, Jenny. So if cheating were a habit with him, he would have done it."

A little tightly, she said, "Are you saying he didn't cheat when he won Belle Retour?"

"I'm saying he probably didn't." Dane's voice was steady. "Men who cheat at cards tend to make a habit of it. Kelly obviously doesn't do that. He's just a very good player."

Jennifer looked blindly through the windshield. So she was left without even that, facing the knowledge that her home had been fairly taken away from her. "Did you cheat to win last night?"

"No."

That answer sounded a little tired, she realized, and she couldn't leave it. "I'm sorry. It's just that I can't forget what you said. That, if the stakes were high enough, you probably would."

Dane was silent for a few minutes, until he turned the Ferrari into the parking lot of a restaurant and stopped. Then he shut off the engine and half turned to look at her. "How high is high enough? That's what you asked once. I've played when the stakes were higher than you can imagine. But I never lost sight of what I was doing. It's just a *game*, Jenny," he said softly.

She looked at him mutely.

"Just a game. A game of cards. A game of skill and tactics and bluff. Stop damning me because I happen to be good at it."

"How can it be just a game to you?" she asked, trying to understand. "You've told me, more than once, that you're a gambler, a professional."

"Yes, I am. But the very fact that I *am* a professional should assure you that I would never risk anything I cared about in a *game.* Would a carpenter live in a badly built house? A race car driver get into a car he knew could fall apart on him? Would you, an artist, deliberately corrupt your talents?"

"You're comparing apples and oranges."

Dane reached for one of her hands, holding it strongly in his own. "No, I'm not. Jenny, you believe that because your father lost everything in a game, your getting involved with me is somehow a danger to you. That I could hurt you the way he did. But you're wrong. You're the one comparing apples and oranges when you compare your father to me. Amateur gamblers are reckless. Professionals aren't."

"You said that every gambler knew one day the stakes might be everything." She kept her voice even.

He carried her hand to his lips and held it there for a brief moment, gazing steadily into her eyes, then held her hand in both his. "That's the point, Jenny. To an amateur gambler, everything *is* everything; he'll stake anything he can call his own, including his home and his self-respect. But to a professional, *everything* is only what he can afford to lose, and that never includes a home—or any harm to someone he loves."

Jennifer could feel his tension as well as her own, but she was still trying to reach an emotional understanding of what he was saying. Her mind acknowledged his meaning, but her heart remembered the pain of her father's betrayal.

"The very skills that made me professional rule out the possibility that I would ever bet what I couldn't afford to lose. Jenny, to me, it's a *game.* A test of skill and concentration. If it ever stops being a game, if the next turn of the card means more to me than the test of those traits, then it'll be the last time I risk anything."

"How can you be so sure?"

"After twenty years? Twenty years, Jenny. Playing cards for fun, for practice, for information, for business. And in all that time, it was only a game I used. Never a game that used me. It never meant more."

"Then why can't you stop?"

"I've been asking myself the same thing during the last few days. And the answer is complicated."

"You won't tell me?"

Dane hesitated, watching her with restless eyes. "Is the reason so important, Jenny? It doesn't change anything. In a way it has to do with something we talked about before. Honor, integrity. If there are any right reasons to become a gambler, then my reasons were right. And if I walk away from it now, I would be saying the last twenty years were meaningless."

Jennifer didn't respond for a long moment. She looked down at his beautiful, long-fingered hands holding hers, conscious of his strain and her own. And in the tangle of her emotions, one thought emerged clearly. *He doesn't have to say this.* He could say gambling meant nothing and that he would give it up if she asked. She would be eager to believe him.

He could have avoided these complications easily, if a relationship with her had meant less than it obviously did to him. But she had been right in believing that there was a core of integrity in him, a basic honesty. He wouldn't tell her what she wanted to hear, because it would be a lie. He wouldn't offer her easy answers, simple solutions, because sometimes the answers aren't simple ones.

It all came down to a question of trust, and he obviously knew that as well as she did. He had tried to assure her, as carefully and reasonably as possible, that he wasn't a *compulsive* gambler, that he would be, by this very professionalism, incapable of a reckless, hurtful act such as her father's. And at no time had he taken advantage of the strong desire they were both constantly aware of in order to sway her to a point beyond reason. He could have, and they both knew it.

"Jenny . . ."

She met his gaze finally, looking into those incredible, vibrant eyes, thinking, *He hasn't made me forget everything but wanting him, and he could . . . he could.* The ache inside her eased. "Do you know that Frost poem, 'The Road Not Taken'?" she asked softly.

He nodded slowly.

With a deep breath, she said, "I haven't had that choice too often in my life, and when I did I took the safe path, with no regrets. But when I met you, the choice wasn't easy anymore. And if I take the safe path this time, I believe I'll always wonder about the one less traveled."

He lifted a hand to her cheek, touching it gently, and suddenly his eyes were like sunlight through purple clouds, lit from within, vivid with promises. "I hope that means what I think it does," he said huskily.

Jennifer smiled, feeling warm and lighter than air. "I thought you were going to feed me."

Seven

Two hours later, Dane and Jennifer were walking together in a park near the restaurant. Since it was summer, the park was alive with children and young people, exploding with activity and laughter. Jennifer thought that Dane had brought her here deliberately, because what he had told her days ago still held true: They would have little time together until he finished his job with Garrett Kelly, and it was clear he had no intention of rushing things between them.

She walked beside him, her hand tucked in the crook of his arm and his hand covering hers, very aware of more than one feminine head turning to get a second glance at Dane. It didn't surprise her. He was a strikingly handsome man of impressive size and grace, and there was a curious aura of dignity and old-world charm about him.

And she felt oddly enclosed by that aura herself. She was conscious that her posture was straighter when she was with him, her head held higher, as if some instinct within her strove to match his innate dignity. As usual he was dressed with semiformality in a cream-colored suit, only the tie missing. As for herself, she was in a casual denim skirt and cotton blouse; she had taken to wearing skirts rather than her usual jeans, even though she had carefully refrained from explaining her motives to herself. But she realized now it was because there was something very *male* about Dane, about that aura of his, something that brought out the feminine in a woman.

Absurdly, she caught herself wishing that hoop skirts and lots of petticoats were still the fashion.

"Riverboats," she murmured to herself.

He looked down at her, smiling. "What?"

Jennifer felt herself flush a little, but she was amused as well. And since they had reached a kind of careful companionship during breakfast, she didn't hesitate to let him know her thoughts now. "I was just thinking how at home you would have looked on a riverboat a hundred years ago." And, as his smile deepened, she added dryly, "You've heard that before."

"Once or twice," he admitted.

She sighed. "If I weren't hanging on your arm, you would have been mobbed by half these women by now."

He laughed, startled. "For God's sake, Jenny!"

"Well, it's true. And you have to know it." She looked up at him, curious. "Don't you?"

"How am I supposed to answer that?" he asked somewhat helplessly.

It was her turn to laugh, but she wasn't willing to drop the subject. "You aren't vain, I know. Most really handsome men are so aware of their looks that's all you remember once they're gone. You aren't like that. And with you . . . it's more than a set of features that happens to be put together well. It's something else. People notice you, no matter where you are or what you're doing, and remember you."

"I'm taller than average," he said dismissively.

Jennifer's amusement increased. He was clearly uncomfortable with the subject, and there was something curiously endearing about that because she knew it was sincere. "That isn't it either," she told him firmly. "But I know what part of it is. You walk like a cat. Or a king."

That really did startle him, and he didn't seem to know whether to laugh or swear. "If you mean I'm arrogant—"

"No, you aren't arrogant." She mused about it, wanting him to understand what it was she saw in him. "Not haughty. Cats and kings have a kind of self-knowledge the rest of us rarely attain. A sure sense of their place in the world. They're centered. Balanced."

A little wryly, he said, "Sure you're talking about me?"

"I'm not saying you don't have doubts from time to time; you wouldn't be human otherwise. It's just that there seems to be something in you that's . . . fixed. Something so deeply certain that it's almost visible. You said you carried your roots around with you. Maybe that's it. The only thing you're tied to is yourself."

He was smiling again, faintly. "What brought on all this analysis?"

They had paused on the path underneath a towering oak, and Jennifer released his arm to wander over and sit on the white bench encircling its girth. "You," she said with a sigh. "And it's your own fault. You've shot my own balance to hell, you know."

"Sorry," he murmured.

She looked at him wryly. "No, you're not."

"All right, then. I'm not sorry. Why should I suffer through this alone?"

"This?" She drew a breath, her amusement vanishing, and added steadily, "We keep dancing around it, don't we?"

Dane stood looking down at her, suddenly grave. "It's too dangerous to stop the music."

Jennifer knew very well that he had been at some pains to keep the music going, to keep things on an even keel between them. And she knew that he was right to think that way as long as their time together had to be brief. There was a wildness they were both conscious of and had little control over, exploding when they touched in anything but a casual way. They were both wary. She felt it in herself, and sensed it in Dane.

But she didn't know what he wanted from her, not completely, and that bothered her. He had never hinted at any kind of a commitment, saying only that he wanted a chance to find out what this was between them. And he had certainly had women throwing themselves at him since his teens. What made her so special that he wouldn't take advantage of obvious desire? What, indeed . . .

Unwilling to continue along those lines, she changed the subject abruptly. "You said you were a gambler and a thief. We haven't talked about the second."

He was silent for a moment, then accepted the change. "It's accurate enough, depending on your point of view. In certain quarters, I have the reputation of being a thief, and I don't deny it. There have been advantages to it."

"As an information broker?" she guessed.

Dane nodded. "Some shady individuals wouldn't talk to me unless I had the reputation I do. It comes in handy."

Jennifer gazed at him steadily. "Reputations don't usually arise out of thin air."

"No. But they can be manufactured."

"The way yours was." It wasn't a question, and Jennifer shook her head a little. "Are you doing it deliberately, Dane?"

"Doing what?"

"Testing me, I suppose. You ask for my trust, yet you're holding back something, keeping a vital piece of the puzzle to yourself. So it must be a test, to see if I can trust you, and maybe even love you."

"It isn't a test, Jenny. There are things I can't tell you yet. Answers I'm not free to give you." He swore softly, looking, in that moment, as if the wildness inside him was threatening to burst free of his careful restraint. "Why the hell do you think I'm being such a bloody gentleman about this? The minute I realized we had something special, I wasn't about to mess it up by rushing you when I couldn't give you all the answers."

"You wanted my eyes wide open," she said softly, because it was a confirmation of what she had only just realized.

Dane didn't seem to hear the new note in her voice. He was clearly struggling to leash what she had so nearly set free. Hands jammed in his pockets, he was standing as if he didn't dare move, as if he wanted badly to move. "I want to take you to bed for a week," he said roughly. "A month. And then it'll be too late for you, Jenny, too late for both of us. I wouldn't be able to let you go after that. So you have to be sure, and you won't be sure without all the answers."

She rose slowly and took a step toward him so that she stood within arm's reach. She could hardly believe what she was feeling, yet she no longer doubted it. And she couldn't take her eyes off him. "It's already too late for me," she told him in a voice she didn't recognize as her own.

Dane didn't move, but in his eyes there was a change, light through a storm, the kind of light that made rainbows. In the distance, the voices and laughter of people and children faded away, put out of reach.

Jennifer could almost hear her heartbeat, and his, and she could feel something inside her give way, all in a rush, as if a wall had collapsed silently. The fears she had been conscious of until then melted away. Into the taut silence, she said softly, "I have all the answers I need, Dane. I think I did from the first. It's just that the wrong questions kept getting in the way."

He half shook his head, an almost unconscious gesture of reluctant negation. "You can't be sure."

"Can't I? These past days, I've been fighting everything I felt, telling myself it couldn't be real. And there were so many questions that it was easy to believe the answers had to be important."

"They are important," he said huskily.

"No. The only important answer is standing in front of me. You. The man you are. All the questions in the world can't keep me from knowing the truth of that answer. You're a man of integrity." She drew a deep breath. "And I love you."

There was an instant of utter stillness, and then Dane was holding her in his arms, tightly, his heart pounding against her. "Thank you," he said quietly into her soft hair.

Jennifer pulled back just far enough to look up at him. "For what?" she asked unsteadily. "For loving you? That was easy. So easy I couldn't believe it."

"For trusting me," he murmured, kissing her gently and then with building desire. "I wasn't sure you could find anything in me to trust, much less—" His voice deepened, as if it came from the core of himself. "I love you, Jenny."

Her arms went up around his neck, and she lost herself in the growing heat of their kiss, feeling a happiness she had never expected to feel. *I love you.* Casual words to some, she knew. Words written in flowing script on greeting cards and sent through the mail. But they weren't casual to her and everything inside her told her they weren't casual to Dane either.

"Oh, damn this job," he muttered suddenly against her lips, then lifted his head to gaze down at her with bright, unshuttered eyes. "God, I'm half out of my mind wanting you, and there just isn't *time.*" His voice was raspy.

Jennifer was staring up into his eyes, and the promises were there again, wild and beckoning, trapped in violet . . . convincing her he did believe there was something special between them, something worth fighting for and preserving. He could so easily have used his sexual power over her, as they both knew he could, and he *hadn't.* He had clung to reason, using only the weapons she could fight, shuttering the incredible force of his remarkable eyes until the fighting was over.

Essences.

"How do you *do* that?" she asked, fascinated.

Dane seemed to find some faint control over the demands of his body, and held on with iron will. He was smiling just a little, something almost sheepish in the curve of his lips. "Do what?" he asked innocently.

She ignored the attempt at ignorance. "You know, dammit. You have to know. It's . . . something I can almost *hear*."

He pulled her arms gently from around his neck and took her hand, beginning to lead her back toward his car with a resolve that was obvious. "As much as I hate to do it, I'd better take you home, and right now. There are some things I have to do before I meet Kelly tonight."

"Dane, I'm not going to let you put me off this time!" She was determined. "I have to know."

He refused to answer until they were in the car and heading back toward her house and even then he seemed reluctant and more than a bit discomfited. "It isn't magic, honey."

"It looks like it from where I'm standing," she told him ruefully. "Please, Dane, tell me."

After a moment, he said, "What did you see?"

"Promises," she answered instantly, half turned in her seat so she could look at him. "Promises I could feel, pulling at me, as if you—as if you knew exactly what I wanted and needed."

Dane reached for her hand and carried it briefly to his lips, then held it firmly on his thigh. "I should have asked you sooner," he said huskily. "It would have been easier for me, knowing that's what you felt. I wasn't sure."

"I don't understand."

"I don't myself, not really." He sent her a quick smile. "I only know I've often been able to sway some people, if I concentrated hard enough. But with you, it was . . . There's so much I want to give you, so many feelings inside wilder than anything I've ever known—"

Jennifer felt her heart turn over when his voice broke off roughly, and her hand tightened in his. "That's what I saw," she said softly. "What I wanted and needed."

Dane was silent for a moment, then said in a thickened voice, "I swear I'll never drive a sports car again."

She thought she knew, but murmured, "Why?"

"Because I want you close beside me from now on," he told her, staring grimly through the windshield in an attempt to keep at least part of his mind on driving. She didn't seem to fully realize the effect she had on him, and he was beyond telling her at the moment. What could he say? That only twenty years of disciplined control over his body, necessary for a successful gambler, made it possible for him to fight the desire to just grab her and carry her off somewhere?

There was so much he wanted to tell her, show her, those wild feelings inside him barely under control. And the ache of his body, present for days now, was a need more powerful than anything he'd ever felt before. The detachment that had for so long been an advantage in his work was gone with her, far out of his reach. He had never considered himself an unfeeling man, but he knew now that he had never felt with the depth and power that loving her made him capable of.

Dear Lord, he loved her. . . .

Sighing unsteadily, Jennifer said, "I'm glad I'm not the only one going crazy."

His laugh was a breath of sound. "Jenny, I passed crazy days ago."

"It doesn't show," she whispered.

He released her hand in the necessity of gearing down and turning the car into her driveway. "Doesn't it?"

Very conscious of his hard thigh under her hand, Jennifer realized that it *did* show. Beneath his composure he was strained, his body tightly wound and feverish. But he was stubbornly determined not to cheat either of them by stealing only a few hours together.

"Damn Kelly!" she muttered with suppressed violence.

Dane stopped the car and then leaned over to kiss her with taut restraint. "I won't get out," he said huskily. "If I put my arms around you one more time, all the good intentions in the world won't be able to stop me."

She fumbled for the door handle and got out of the car slowly, feeling hot and restless and more than a little dazed. "You're sure it'll be over tonight with Kelly?"

"I'll make sure of it."

Jennifer didn't question, but merely nodded and stepped back, closing the Ferrari's door and drawing away from it. She watched the car pull out of the driveway and start back toward Lake Charles, watched until she could no longer see it. Then she went into the house.

She found herself alone for the day, Francesca having left a note to remind her of her weekly lunch-and-bridge arrangement with old friends. Jennifer was relieved that her mother was gone; her feelings for Dane were new and wondrous, and she wanted to hold them close to herself for a while until they became more familiar.

If they ever did.

It wasn't only her love for him that was unfamiliar, but herself as well. She felt curiously raw, sensitive to everything around her as if her very flesh was new and tender. Butterflies, she thought, must feel that way, wings unfurling and still damp from the chrysalis, vulnerable, susceptible to untold damage in the first vital moments after their transformation.

She felt like that, exposed in a new form she hardly recognized. Some rigidity in herself she had barely been aware of when it existed was gone now, leaving her softened, almost undefined. All the emotions Dane had drawn to the surface remained there, and she didn't feel the need to fight them any longer.

Jennifer tried to work in her study, but found it a wasted effort. More than once, she caught herself gazing into space, her mind filled with images having nothing to do with work. Finally, abandoning the struggle, she left the room. It was after two o'clock; she had skipped lunch, but wasn't hungry.

Nothing in the house could hold her attention for long, and by three o'clock she was too restless to remain there. She decided to walk to Belle Retour, nothing in mind but her need to be active and her desire to look at the lost home that was still a bittersweet ache inside her. She would merely look, she assured herself, going no farther than the woods near the house. Just stand and look and, perhaps, this time manage to say good-bye.

She had forgotten Dane's promise.

The path she took, one she had made herself over the years when the cottage had been her studio, cut the two-mile distance to the house almost in half. Not yet overgrown, it wound through the woods and along the edges of fields. She walked slowly, enjoying the warm breeze, thinking vaguely that a storm was coming. After growing up here in an area vulnerable to fierce gulf storms, she had become like a cat in her sensitivity to the falling air pressure that heralded a storm, and that instinct told her now that the pressure was low, and dropping.

Was a storm forecast, perhaps even a hurricane? This was the season for them, but Jennifer hadn't paid attention to weather reports on radio or television lately. Her pace quickened even as the breeze died, and she knew without thinking about it that a storm was no more than an hour away.

There was still time, she thought.

She found herself on the edge of the woods no more than a hundred yards from the house, and stood gazing toward it, conscious of a tangle of emotions. Odd, she thought, that this old collection of bricks and wood could rouse such feelings, inspire such memories. . . .

Her mind snapped back to the present as she watched Garrett Kelly emerge from a side door and start out through the garden, and she frowned in puzzlement. He was carrying a small satchel made of leather, and his step was brisk. And he didn't stop when he got through the overgrown garden, but continued into the woods to the south of the house.

Where was he going? she wondered uneasily. There was nothing in that direction except—

Of course! The realization was stark in her mind, and she couldn't believe she hadn't thought of it sooner. Where else could a man hope to hide a printing press—

even an entire counterfeiting operation—except in the depths of an almost inaccessible cypress swamp?

Jennifer surveyed the house and grounds quickly, looking around intently, but saw no sign that Kelly was being followed. Where was Dane's partner? This was what they'd been waiting for, what this entire operation had come down to, and there was no one following Kelly!

She hesitated, biting her bottom lip in indecision, then swore softly and started out after him. She was hardly dressed for a trek into the swamp, but there was no time to worry about that. She'd just have to trust to her own surefootedness and keep a wary eye out for snakes. In her tomboy days, she had practically lived in the swamp—to the despair of Francesca—and there were few who knew it as well as she did.

So Jennifer trusted herself to find out just where Kelly was going; she thought she could even guess now. She didn't look back as she vanished into the forest, which was a pity. If she had, she would have seen a tall man step from the concealing shadows near the house and stare after her, a frown on his face. She might even have heard him utter a variation of her earlier cussword with a great deal more force. But she didn't look back.

Instead, Jennifer concentrated on speed until she caught a glimpse of Kelly ahead of her, then settled down to match his pace and be quiet about it. There was no path through these woods, at least none to speak of, but she saw evidence that Kelly had gone this way more than once in the past. She felt a surge of excitement, increasingly certain that she was right.

And she was so conscious of the prey ahead of her, that she never noticed the silent hunter behind her.

The ground beneath her feet became softer and wetter as they neared the swamp, the towering oak trees thinning out and gradually becoming the cypress trees common in such an area. It became more difficult to keep close to Kelly, and Jennifer was forced to drop back in order to hide her own presence as the concealing underbrush of the forest gave way and the rich, ripe smell of wetlands closed around her.

She glanced up once to find the sky leaden, conscious of increasing heat, of stillness. Definitely a storm, and probably a big one. She realized only then that Kelly was unlikely to have run an electric line out here. Did he have a generator? Was his press electric? And why, she wondered suddenly, had Dane found in the safe only one of the necessary two plates?

Some part of her mind turning those questions over, she followed Kelly cautiously, skirting the edge of the swamp where it was almost literally impassible, where murky water ringed tall cypress trees and rotting stumps alike. Broken-off trees reared up like jagged wooden teeth, and limbs floated idly on the still water.

Jennifer hardly noticed the eerie landscape, too intent on her quarry. She followed him to an old shack on the far edge of the swamp, watched him enter the ramshackle building. After an instant's hesitation, she crept closer, as silent as possible, until she could crouch below a boarded-up window at the side of the house.

Hearing another man's voice, she managed a quick look between the boards, surprised to realize that the other man had been living in the shack, and for some time it appeared. She could barely see a narrow cot, a shelf with foodstuffs, a small table.

And an old printing press.

Elated, Jennifer pressed her ear close to the wood and listened, determined to find out all she could. For the first fifteen minutes or so, she heard only the low murmur of voices, indistinguishable, droning on. It was impossible to catch more than a word here and there. Then the voices rose in anger, and she heard very clearly what was going on.

"So it's all right when *you* need money," the stranger was saying bitterly.

"Listen to me," Kelly told him in a hard voice. "If you hadn't gone crazy and spent thousands right here in the area, we wouldn't have had to lie low for a while at all. I've told you, we'll be back in business in a few weeks, once we're sure they can't trace those bills back to us."

"And what about this? You want me to print out half a million so you can play poker with some cardsharp!"

"I gave him a note, don't you get it? The only way I can redeem it is with phony bills."

"Oh, hell, why don't you just tell him you don't have the money? Let him sue you for it."

"Fool." Kelly paused, obviously gathering the threads of his patience. "He's a professional gambler, Alan, and men like that don't go to court to collect poker debts."

"Afraid of a busted kneecap?" Alan sneered.

Kelly ignored the question and the sneer. "I have to redeem that note. And Prescott has three quarters of a million to lose."

"He hasn't lost yet," Alan reminded bitterly.

"He will. Tonight. I mean to beat him."

"And what if you don't? What if he walks away from the table with half a million in phony money? We'll have the feds down on us so fast—"

"Don't be stupid. He's going back to Florida after this last game. Besides, money passes through his hands so quickly that even if he found out it was phony he'd never know where it came from. We're covered even if I lose. But I won't."

Alan was silent for a moment, then said flatly, "You'd better win from the first hand then, because you won't have half a million to play with."

"What?"

"You heard me. We suspended operations, remember? I have just enough paper here to print about a hundred and fifty grand. And our paper supplier's in Baton Rouge."

"Damn," Kelly said softly and bitterly.

"Still think you can beat him?" Alan jeered.

"Just print the money. How long?"

"With or without serial numbers?"

"How long, dammit?"

"A few hours."

"I'll come back then."

"Listen," Alan said suddenly, "are you sure that cousin of yours won't tip the feds? You said he had the plate."

"He won't turn me in." Dryly, Kelly added, "He may try to blackmail me later, but we'll deal with that if and when it happens."

Alan grunted.

Jennifer heard the sudden creak of the door being opened, and flattened herself against the shack to avoid being seen. Kelly would turn in the opposite direction when he left, she knew, which meant he wouldn't see her—

Then, her mind fixed on Kelly, she abruptly felt more than heard another presence, and before she could move, a hand was clamped firmly over her mouth.

Dane had managed to sleep a couple of hours, and awoke feeling far more rested than he'd expected. He showered and shaved, and was about to start making calls to find someone who knew a bit about presses when the phone rang.

It was Skye, calling from the phone he always insisted on in a rental car.

"Better get out here," he said without preamble. "Our man just struck off through the woods with a bag, and Jennifer's trailing behind him."

"Damn!"

"I said something stronger than that," Skye told him. "She's being cautious, so it may be all right. I'll keep them both in sight, but according to maps of the area, they're headed into a swamp."

Dane looked at his watch, thinking rapidly. "It'll take me about fifteen minutes to get there."

Skye didn't question the optimistic estimate; he knew how fast Dane drove. "Come in from the southwest," he said. "Assuming they've reached their destination by then, I'll meet you about halfway along that old track from the main road to the house. If I'm not there, head east to the swamp."

"On my way," Dane said. He wasted no time on the drive, settling the Ferrari into its highest gear and hurtling around curves in a way that made the tires whine. Fifteen minutes after leaving his hotel, he was parked on Belle Retour land, out of the car, and heading through the woods.

Both partners had a strong sense of direction, and neither was surprised when they encountered each other near the edge of the swamp. Skye had been moving back away from the swamp and toward the track, but halted and waited for Dane to reach him.

"Where is she?" Dane asked immediately, keeping his voice low with an effort.

"Calm down, she's fine," Skye told him. "Kelly went into a shack on the other side of the swamp, and she's settled down right next to it, listening. Someone's been living in the shack, by the way, one man."

"That may explain why Kelly has only one plate," Dane said absently as they began working their way cautiously toward the swamp. "If he has a partner, each of them could hold one plate until they print."

"To make sure nobody gets too greedy," Skye mused. "It figures. Crooks do tend to think that way."

Thunder rumbled suddenly, and Dane glanced up at the sky, frowning. "A storm. That's all we need."

His partner didn't comment, but led the way around the edge of the swamp until they were in a position to see the shack clearly, and Jennifer's still form crouched beneath a boarded-up window.

"She's too close," Dane muttered.

"Not unless she makes a noise."

Dane shook his head. "I won't take the chance. Look, you stick with Kelly if he leaves before I get Jenny out of here."

"What about the press?"

"If Kelly leaves, follow him. I doubt he'll bolt, but we

don't need to take chances now. I'll take care of the press if I can. If it comes down to a choice between disabling the press or getting Jenny safely out of here, to hell with the press."

Skye nodded, but said flatly, "Don't risk your skin to get at the press."

Dane left his partner's side, moving cautiously and trying to keep under cover as long as possible. Still, he was forced to cross a good twenty feet of open area in order to get to Jennifer, and he was halfway across that when the shack's door began to creak open. He covered the last ten feet with a speed that would have surprised him if he'd been conscious of it, and clamped a hand firmly over Jennifer's mouth just as Kelly stepped out of the shack and shoved the door closed behind him.

She stiffened against him for a brief moment, then relaxed suddenly, but Dane didn't release her until he was sure Kelly was well on his way back to the house.

"Fancy meeting you here," Jennifer said in a breathless whisper.

Eight

Dane hugged her wordlessly for a moment, grateful that she would emerge from this unharmed. From the moment he had heard Kelly had a partner, he had known that there must indeed be a counterfeit operation of some scope, and that meant Kelly and his partner would have a great deal to lose. Men in such positions tended to protect their interests, often with violence.

Jennifer could have gotten herself killed.

He waited until sounds from inside the shack indicated the occupant was busy and less apt to hear them, then caught Jennifer's hand and drew her back across the clearing and into the partial cover of a trio of cypress trees.

"What the hell are you doing, Jenny?" he muttered.

She kept her voice low as well. "I suddenly realized where the press had to be, so I followed him to make sure. There was nobody else—"

"Skye was watching him, Jenny. My partner."

"I didn't see him."

"You weren't supposed to," Dane told her dryly.

She smiled reluctantly. "I didn't think of that. I'm sorry, Dane. But it's all right after all. And the press is in there. I saw it."

He glanced toward the shack, frowning. "I need to get in," he said half to himself.

Jennifer held on to his hand tightly. "You can't. It's too dangerous. There's another man, and he didn't sound very nice."

Dane hesitated, still frowning. "Could you tell if it was an electric press?"

"Manual. An old one."

"Damn. And I'll bet Kelly told his partner to print out anything up to a million bucks."

Jennifer wasn't sure why it mattered, but she was glad her reckless action was providing information Dane would find useful. "That's what he wanted, but the other man—Kelly called him Alan—told him there wasn't enough paper for that much. He said he could print only a hundred and fifty thousand."

Some of Dane's tension eased, and he sent a mental thanks to Lady Luck. "Good. Now, come on. I'm getting you out of here."

"Wait." Jennifer's attention had been caught by a flicker of movement between them and their path back toward the house, and she looked in that direction now. "We can't go back the same way. Look over there."

He followed her gaze to their left, his eyes narrowing on a ten-foot-long grayish shape that had crawled from the water and onto a hummock of damp earth. It was an alligator, and it didn't look at if it had any intention of moving in the near future. And it was perched on the only patch of reasonably dry land in that direction, with murky water all around.

"He probably wouldn't attack us," Jennifer said slowly. "They don't usually bother people. But . . ."

"But," Dane agreed dryly. He looked back over his shoulder at the thickening woods behind them. "How about that way?"

She was shaking her head. "This swamp is fed by an offshoot of the Calcasieu River. If we go that way, we'll have to cross it, and after all the rain we've had lately, we'd have to circle all the way back to the main road to find a safe way across."

Dane looked to his right, studying the eerie landscape of the swamp. "Can we circle the swamp that way?"

"It'll take more than an hour to work our way around," she told him. "But it passable and safer."

He looked at her with a smile. "I gather you know this godforsaken place like the back of your hand?"

"I practically grew up here," she said, returning his smile. "We used to play games in the swamp."

He shook his head a little, but said, "You lead the way, then."

Holding his hand, Jennifer led the way, taking them toward the east and working her way carefully along a path she remembered from childhood. The swamp had changed since then, of course, and she found herself forced to search for alternate paths from time to time because a fallen tree that had once been a bridge had rotted and collapsed into the water, or because a remembered hummock was now beneath the surface.

She led them without flinching past a second alligator, and paused once as a water moccasin slithered by no more than two feet away. Dane, watching her, was fascinated by her composure. He knew that there was no particular virtue in accepting what was familiar—and this swamp was definitely familiar to Jennifer. Still, the recklessness of youth almost always gave way to the cautious awareness of adulthood, and more than one childish bravery became a fear in later years.

But not with Jennifer. She had true courage, he thought, the kind of courage that was instinctive and unaware, that accepted small dangers and large ones without thought. He had known that already, though. She loved him—and how much courage had been demanded of her to take that risk?

Within fifteen minutes, they were completely out of sight of the shack Kelly had led them to, and the scents and sounds of the swamp closed around them like a hot, wet blanket. It was darker now, the tall trees all around blocking most of the sky.

Jennifer paused, looking around slowly, and Dane felt it the moment she did. Stillness. An abrupt silence as if all the birds and animals of the swamp had suddenly become mute. He hadn't realized how many sounds had filled the air until they were gone, leaving a thick, heavy silence behind.

"A storm," Jennifer said, her tone normal now that they were far from listening ears. "And a bad one, I think. We'll never make it around the swamp in time." She looked at him, hesitated. "I know a place about five minutes from here, shelter. But we may be stuck there for hours."

Dane glanced at his watch, mentally calculating. After four now; he had promised to play the final game with Kelly sometime around nine tonight. He wasn't particularly concerned about being late. The storm could serve as an excuse if he needed one. And Skye wouldn't expect to see him until he saw him. "Let's go for it," he told Jennifer.

She led the way, angling slightly away from the swamp and into the forest of mixed oak, elm and cypress trees. The footing beneath them gradually became more secure, though still damp. Thunder rumbled more insistently now, and in the trees above a sudden wind snatched at the leaves and branches.

The rain hit them when they were still more than twenty yards from a small structure that appeared little more sturdy than Kelly's shack, and by the time they pushed open the door and lurched inside they were both soaked.

Dane forced the door shut behind them, leaning into it because of the building gusts of wind, and when the door finally caught he turned to find Jennifer lighting a kerosene lamp. The room had been pitch dark due to wooden shutters fastened securely over the two windows.

"Welcome to Narna's home," she said somewhat breathlessly.

He looked around, surprised to find the place much more comfortable than he'd expected. There was a polished wooden table and two chairs in the single room, along with a narrow cot half hidden behind a startling and garish Chinese screen over five feet tall and at least that wide. Woven rugs dotted the wood floor, along with a thick, fluffy one before the hearth, and the fireplace was made of river rock, with a generous supply of cut wood and kindling stacked beside it. Shelves lined one wall, holding enigmatically labeled glass jars and cans of food, and a couple of cabinets hid whatever they contained. There as an old iron stove, cold and black, and bright orange curtains at both windows.

"Who's Narna?" Dane asked, conscious of both the damp and a surprising chill in the room.

"She's a Cajun witch-woman."

Dane stared at her. "You're kidding."

Jennifer solemnly returned his incredulous gaze. "Seriously. She's lived on the edge of the swamp for thirty years. Dad tried to relocate her half a dozen times, but finally gave up. Her presence here generally keeps poachers out of the swamp. The people around here believe the place is cursed. Kelly couldn't have picked a better spot to hide his press."

"*Is* the place cursed?"

"Depends on your point of view. Since everybody believes it and stays away—just what Narna wanted— then I suppose you could call it cursed."

"You've been here before," Dane noted.

"Sure. I told you I practically grew up in and around the swamp. Narna and I've been friends for years." Gravely, she added, "I even came to her when I was twelve to get a potion to make a boy fall in love with me."

"Did it work?"

"He carried my books for a semester after that. It didn't last, though. Love never does when you're twelve."

Abruptly conscious of how her blouse clung wetly to the rich curves beneath it, Dane cleared his throat and yanked his gaze away from her to the fireplace. "Would Narna mind if I built a fire? It's chilly in here."

"She wouldn't mind." Jennifer hesitated, then stepped out of her ruined sandals and headed toward the folding screen by the cot. "I'm going to get out of these wet clothes," she said steadily. "You should get out of yours, too."

Concentrating on building the fire, Dane fought the urge to agree with her. He reminded himself with all the force he could muster that Jennifer didn't know the truth of his life yet, didn't know that he was deeply committed to his masquerade. She didn't even know there *was* a masquerade, and he couldn't explain yet. Until he could . . .

His white shirt stuck to him uncomfortably. He had left the hotel in such a hurry that he hadn't put on a jacket or tie, so both his shirt and undershirt had been soaked in the downpour. He didn't trust himself to remove even the top shirt, but he did take a moment to pull off his drenched shoes and socks, and set them to one side.

"Where is Narna now?" he managed to ask, feeding kindling into the flames his lighter had ignited.

"In Seattle with her sister," Jennifer called back easily. "She hates this place in the summer."

Dane glanced up as a rumble of thunder and accompanying gust of wind shook the structure. "I don't blame her. Are you sure her house can hold up under a storm?"

"Very sure. It's stood for thirty years, and weathered several hurricanes. We're safe enough."

He listened to the storm raging outside, hoping she was right. The fire was crackling loudly now, and he piled several of the cut logs over the kindling until it burned steadily. Then, restless, he rose to his feet and wandered over to look at the shelves, trying not to think of Jennifer taking her clothes off behind the flimsy screen on the other side of the small room.

"There should be at least a bottle of wine and some glasses in that cabinet to your right," she said.

Her voice was closer now, but he didn't turn to look at her. Instead, he opened the cabinet indicated, finding the wine and a number of delicate glasses.

"This is a very strange place," he muttered.

Jennifer half laughed, draping her clothes over the back of a chair to dry before moving to sink down on the thick rug in front of the hearth. She had wrapped the quilt from the cot around her, and felt more than a little vulnerable. "You mean because of the odd mixture of things?" she asked, keeping her voice light with an effort. "It's very like Narna, that mixture. Kerosene lamps and iron stoves, along with delicate glasses and bright colors."

"And love potions on the shelf," he said, having noticed a particular label.

"Maybe I should put some of that into your wine," she murmured. "It worked when I was twelve." She tried to laugh, but it didn't quite come off.

Dane turned toward her, holding the bottle and two glasses, and went still when he saw her. She seemed impossibly fragile, wrapped in a colorful quilt, the firelight flickering over her bare shoulders and exquisite face. She was defenseless, a vulnerable curve to her lips, eyes shadowed. Her golden hair, drying in the heat of the fire, fell over her shoulders in burnished waves.

After a moment, Dane went over and sank down beside her on the rug, not quite touching her. He uncorked the wine bottle and poured ruby liquid into the two glasses. Setting the bottle aside, he handed her one glass and took the other himself. "Jenny, do you doubt that I love you?"

"No." But the glance she sent him was uncertain. She sipped her wine, adding, "I know this business with Kelly is more important right now—"

"No, it isn't." He swore softly. "Not more important. It's just that you don't know the whole story, and until you do . . ."

"What?" She turned her head to look at him. "Are you so sure these answers of yours are going to make a difference, Dane? How could they?"

He was silent for a moment, then said roughly, "Could you live with a gambler, Jenny?"

"With you, yes," she answered simply.

He wanted to ask, *Can you live with secrets? With lies and deceptions? Not between us—but all around us? Could you love me even in the face of that?* But he couldn't ask; a promise kept him silent, and he had never broken a promise.

"Dane?"

"I don't want you to regret anything, honey, that's all." He kept his voice even.

She was incredulous. "How could I regret loving you?"

He set his glass aside, his hands lifting to frame her

face. "I think I'd die if that happened," he said huskily, gazing into her shadowed blue eyes. "I think that's what I'm afraid of."

"It won't happen." She put her own glass aside blindly, both her hands lifting to his broad chest. Without even thinking about it, she began unbuttoning his damp shirt, her fingers nimble despite the tremors that shook them. "I love you, Dane. I could never regret it."

He was still for a moment, then bent his head and kissed her. Gently at first, his lips toyed with hers, seductive and not quite teasing. His tongue glided along the sensitive inner surface of her lips, and her cool mouth opened to him, heating under the increasing demand of his.

Jennifer felt his hands slip down to her bare shoulders, while her own coped with the remaining buttons of his shirt and tugged it free of his pants. She was lost in the taste of him, wine-sweet and drugging, caught by the heat emanating from his big, hard body and almost burning her. She was barely aware of the storm outside, of thunder and lightning and wind and the harsh rattle of rain on the tin roof.

She was aware only of him, and of the building fire trapped within them both.

She felt him shrug the unbuttoned shirt off and toss it aside, and his mouth lifted from hers so that he could peel the undershirt off over his head. Her hands touched his bare chest almost tentatively, her senses flaring at the erotic brush of hair, and she looked at him through dazed eyes, conscious of an almost primitive shock. Because he was invariably semiformally dressed, she was somehow surprised by the powerful, hair-roughened expanse of his chest.

His half-naked body made her mouth go dry, her throat tighten, and she could scarcely breathe. He was beautiful in a way she'd never known a man could be, in a way that tugged at everything female in her, making her acutely aware of her own body. The black hair covering his chest was almost a pelt, thick and soft beneath her fingers, and she could see his power now in the hard muscles padding his tanned shoulders and cording his forearms.

He could break her, she realized vaguely, her trembling fingers compulsively stroking over his chest, his ribs and hard, flat stomach. He had a kind of natural physical strength that few men could boast, the kind that would require a conscious effort to temper. No wonder he was so calm and almost lazy on the surface, she thought. He had to be so controlled, because if he ever allowed himself a physical outlet for strong emotions . . .

"Jenny?" he questioned huskily, unmoving, his hands holding her shoulders gently.

She lifted her gaze to the vivid sheen of his eyes, realizing that he had seen her instinctive shock. But her trust in him was complete, and after the first jolt she felt no fear of his strength, no wariness or uncertainty. Her arms wreathed his neck and she rose on her knees, her slender body pressing against him, only the quilt still encircling her separating them above the waist.

"I love you," she whispered against his lips.

Dane's arms wrapped around her, hard but gentle, holding her tightly against him. His mouth slanted across hers, deepening the contact between them, his tongue invading, possessing.

Jennifer felt herself being eased back onto the soft hearthrug, and an unconscious murmur of protest came throatily from her when his mouth lifted from hers. But then she opened her eyes and looked up at him, and what she saw in his face stole what little remaining breath she could claim. She had never seen such hunger in a man, such intensity, his eyes were alive with it and fixed on her face as if nothing else in the world mattered.

His big hands went to the quilt and pulled it gently from around her, opening the covering as if she were some gift brightly wrapped in shining paper, a delicate thing to be treasured. A hoarse, raw sound escaped him when she lay naked beside him, the firelight flickering over her slender but richly curved body, and his hand shook a little as it slid up over her ribs to cup a full, aching breast.

"God, you're beautiful," he said in a rasping voice so low she just barely heard it.

She gasped at the shock of pleasure as he touched her, and when the rough pad of his thumb brushed her tightening nipple she felt an explosion of heat inside her. She clutched his shoulders wildly, her senses spinning, only a fire of need inside her to fill the growing ache of emptiness. Then his mouth was on her, sliding hotly over her feverish skin, wringing a wordless cry from her when it captured her nipple. The swirling caress of his tongue sent waves of pleasure through her, and she could hardly bear to be still in the restless storm of her desire.

Jennifer had never realized her body was capable of such feelings. She was dizzy with the clash of pleasure and torment, and she would have asked why he was doing this to her if she could have found the breath for it. Dimly, she heard soft sounds, like the murmurs of a kitten, sounds that seemed to inflame him even more as his mouth became rougher, the hands stroking over her body more insistent.

It occurred to her only vaguely that the sounds were coming from her.

She could feel one of his hands moving along her thighs with a sure, enticing touch, until her legs parted for him, and her body arched in a helpless reaction when his fingers settled gently over the empty ache between them. She thought her entire body was pulsing, a quickening heartbeat of need, and his slow, steady caress was driving her out of her mind.

His mouth moved from one breast to the other, hungry, the touch maddening her until her nails bit into his shoulders and she writhed with a moan. Tension built inside her, winding tighter and tighter, and her body belonged to someone else, not to her, because she couldn't control it.

"Dane . . ." she managed shakily in a voice that almost wasn't there, certain that she was dying because feelings this intense could only demand death as their price. But she was unable to say more than his name, only a wild cry torn from her throat as the tension snapped violently and waves of mind-numbing pleasure swept over her.

In the stunned aftermath of that explosion, she lay limply trying to catch her breath, aware of his movement as he stripped the remainder of his clothing off and tossed it aside. Then his mouth and hands were on her once more, breathing on the embers of her passion until she was burning again, pulsing anew with a need that was even deeper and stronger than before.

The unfamiliar response of her body had blinded her before, but now she could sense and feel Dane's desire, and that awareness sent her own hunger soaring. His big, powerful body was shaking, his skin so hot it was as if a mortal fever raged inside him. And his eyes, his beautiful eyes, were luminous and fierce, intent on her face, her body.

Jennifer almost sobbed aloud when he finally rose above her, and she cradled his body eagerly, the smooth slide of his hard hips against her inner thighs a new and welcome caress. She felt a blunt pressure against her wet flesh, and then her body was yielding, accepting him with an ease that almost shocked her; it was as if she had been waiting for him, for this. The emptiness inside her was filling with him, with the heat and throbbing power of him, and she arched up instinctively to have more of him, all of him.

An inarticulate groan rasped from Dane's throat, and his face tightened in a spasm of intense pleasure. "Lord, Jenny," he whispered roughly, his hands tangling in her hair as he bore her back down into the quilt and rug, kissing her deeply.

She probed his shoulders and back compulsively, her mouth wild under his as he began moving inside her. What she had felt before was nothing compared to this, and she was totally unprepared for the shattering sensations of joining that were so starkly intimate she could only accept them with wonder and a madly escalating excitement.

Heat built inside her with every powerful thrust of his body, until she couldn't stand it any longer. He caught her wordless cry with his mouth, his ragged groan mingling with her softer whimper, burying himself within her as pleasure jolted through them both like shock waves.

He was a big man, and heavy, but Jennifer was conscious of no discomfort as her heart slowed, her breathing steadied. She slid her palms up over his back and shoulders, loving the feel of his damp bronze skin, the hard muscles that were relaxed now. His fingers were still threaded through her hair, moving caressingly against her scalp, and she wanted to arch her back like a cat in the warm, sleepy aftermath of pleasure.

Dane eased up onto his elbows and kissed her, a long, slow, deep kiss that seemed to brand her indelibly, and when he lifted his head again, his eyes were brilliant. "I love you, Jenny," he murmured, the words rumbling from deep inside him.

"I love you too," she told him huskily.

"You'd better." His mouth was curved in a smile that was faintly humorous and heart-stoppingly male. "You couldn't keep me away from you now with a loaded gun."

Jennifer, usually prickly where her independence was concerned, found herself thoroughly enjoying his possessiveness. Smiling unconsciously, she said, "Are you going to be a jealous lover?"

"Smile like that at another man and I will be." He

laughed softly, a sound edged with a kind of surprise. "I can't seem to control my instincts where you're concerned."

"What instincts are those?" she asked innocently.

"The ones born in the cave." His fingers tightened in her hair, lifting her head up for another of those deep, drugging kisses. In a rough voice, he muttered against her lips, "How can a woman so delicate and ladylike as you are make me feel like some half-tamed animal?"

"I don't know, but I love it." Her eyes gleamed up at him, the darkened sheen of them catching and reflecting the firelight. One of her hands glided up his spine, making the muscles of his back ripple in a strong response, and her smile widened as he caught his breath. "A lion in summer," she murmured throatily, "black-maned and beautiful. That's what you are, Dane. A cat . . . and a king." Her eyes began to close as she felt the stirring renewal of need, and her body instinctively held him more tightly.

Dane caught his breath again, his entire body reacting wildly to that hot inner caress, moving against her and inside her with a compulsion he wasn't about to fight. Only the sharp edge of his need for her had been blunted, and he lost himself now in the silken heat of her body.

They were both reluctant to return to other demands on them, but the storm outside died at last, like the fire in the hearth, and it was time for them to leave.

"It'll be dark within an hour," Jennifer said, standing in the open doorway, fully dressed. "Won't your partner be worried about you?"

Dane came up behind her and wrapped his arms around her, resting his chin on the top of her head. "No," he replied. "He'll know I'm not in trouble."

"How?" she asked curiously.

He hesitated, then said, "We were both out there at Kelly's shack. Skye followed Kelly back to the house."

She accepted the explanation, then said, "It'll be over tonight? You're sure of that?"

"Yes."

"Why do you have to play against him now? Since you know where the press is, I mean."

"It'll be easier to make a case against him if he tries to pass some of that phony money," Dane said lightly. He hugged her tightly, then sighed and released her. "We'd better go while there's still enough light to see the snakes and alligators," he told her wryly.

Jennifer hated leaving, but she couldn't argue with what he had said; the swamp could be a dangerous place, especially in the dark. So they tidied Narna's small home and set out to circumvent the swamp in order to return to the main grounds of Belle Retour. It took nearly an hour to make their way to where Dane had left the Ferrari hidden on the track near the lane, and by then it was dark.

Dane had to return to his hotel to change before meeting Kelly, so he drove Jennifer to her house. He quite literally didn't have the time to linger, but made one very expressive comment as she was getting out of the car after the most passionate leave-taking they could manage under the circumstances.

"Sports cars," he grumbled.

Jennifer had to laugh, even though she felt annoyed herself at those damned bucket seats and the gear box between.

"I'll be back in the morning," he told her.

She nodded. "I'll be here."

After the car was out of sight, she wandered into the house, and found her mother standing, hands on her hips, just inside the door. "Well?" Francesca demanded.

Jennifer, very conscious of wrinkled clothing and what she suspected was a permanent smile on her face, blinked and tried to look innocent. "Well, what?"

"When is this man going to marry you?" her mother asked in a fine show of maternal niceties.

"Well, since he hasn't asked me—"

"I will speak to him," Francesca decided.

"You will not," Jennifer told her fiercely. "And stop calling him *this man*. His name is Dane, and I love him." In a defiant tone, she added, "And if he doesn't want to marry me, I'll still love him, and I'll live with him wherever he wants!"

Tempestuously, Francesca threw her arms around her daughter and hugged her, laughing aloud. "Ah, you *do* love him! Will he take care of you, my baby?"

"Yes," Jennifer answered without a shadow of doubt. "He makes me happy, Mother."

Francesca looked at her intently. "And his gambling? That no longer disturbs you?"

Jennifer smiled slowly. "I love a man who happens to be very good at playing a game. So good, in fact, that he's become a professional. I'm not afraid of that anymore."

Her mother pursed her lips unconsciously. She studied Jennifer with an appraising eye and then, decisively, said, "You will have beautiful babies together, I think."

Remembering the passionate interlude in Narna's shack, Jennifer felt herself flush a little. "No doubt," she murmured.

"I will be a grandmother." Francesca turned this new idea over, half winced, then shrugged away what was obviously a disconcerting realization. "I shall learn to knit," she said in a brave tone.

Jennifer giggled despite herself.

Francesca eyed her sternly. "Grandmothers do that," she explained quite unnecessarily.

"You aren't a grandmother yet," Jennifer reminded her. "And stop building families, will you please? Dane might well have a thing or two to say about his future, you know."

"He loves children," Francesca said complacently.

"How do you know?"

"He told me."

Jennifer thought about that, remembering Dane's brief visit with her mother days before. Her eyes narrowed suspiciously. "After you innocently asked him, I suppose?"

"A mother must know these things, my baby." Francesca was unrepentant.

Half closing her eyes, Jennifer sighed. "It's a wonder he didn't kick up dust getting out of here," she murmured. "Dane is a brave man, Mother. A very brave man."

"Of course. A man in love is always brave." But Francesca's voice was absent. Clearly, her volatile mind was angling toward another subject. "Our Belle, Jennifer. Will we get our Belle back again?"

Jennifer hesitated, then said, "Kelly will go to jail, thanks to Dane. But I don't know about Belle, Mother."

Characteristically, Francesca didn't request an explanation. "He should be shot, that Kelly," she said roundly.

Jennifer went suddenly still, remembering something. A promise. Dane had made her a promise. Slowly, she said, "One last game."

"What, my baby?"

"Nothing." Jennifer was unwilling to raise false hopes. But her heart was beating fast, and she wondered.

Nine

"I'll hold the I.O.U. until after the game, if you like," Dane offered easily. "We can settle up then."

An almost imperceptible tension eased from Garrett Kelly's expression. "Fine. And I hope you brought plenty of money. I mean to take it tonight."

"You can certainly try," Dane told him, his tone still light. "And you wouldn't be the first to do it."

They were back in the parlor, sitting on either side of the green baize game table. As they were alone this time, it was one against one, skill against skill. On the mantel, the clock ticked steadily; otherwise, the house was silent.

The game began quietly, reasonable bets made in an almost casual manner. But beneath the surface, Kelly was taut. And Dane was aware that he himself was too tired for this, not at his best. Still, he was determined to get Jennifer's home back for her, and he understood the legal system too well to believe there was a better way than this.

The danger was that this way presented more than its share of drawbacks. After twenty years, Dane understood the game too well to discount sheer, blind luck as a factor, and that could work to Kelly's benefit as easily as to his own. But he had already made up his mind to win fairly—if Kelly played fairly.

And, as the hours passed, it became obvious to Dane that his opponent was not cheating.

Dane played with no change in his serene expression, losing some hands, winning most. He watched the money come and go on the table, Kelly's phony bills mixing with his own legal ones. And, just as the night before, he was waiting for Kelly to become a little too intense, a little too willing to believe in his own luck. It was a common gambler's fever, that state—and exactly what had happened to Jennifer's father.

Inevitably, it was happening to Kelly tonight.

The game went on, and Dane casually accepted more of Kelly's I.O.U.s, making certain that the other man won back the scraps of paper each time he was driven to scrawl another one, even if Dane had to fold with a winning hand to do it. He expected Kelly to begin using the promises of payment as actual money, staking them over and over just as he would cash, and that was exactly what Kelly did. But whenever Dane took a pot containing a scrap of paper with the other man's promise scrawled on it, he set it casually to one side and didn't bet with it himself.

"Call. Raise two thousand."

"Your two. And two more."

"Call."

"Four queens."

"Damn."

With the sure skill of a hunter, Dane made certain that Kelly was never completely out of the game, that he never abandoned hope of coming out ahead. Concentrating intently, and having gained an insight into the mannerisms of the other man after several nights of play, Dane unerringly knew when Kelly was holding a strong hand, or when he was bluffing, and he used that knowledge carefully.

The scraps of paper at his elbow increased, apparently unnoticed by Kelly. Like many gamblers, the intensity of the play blinded him to his own growing debts, and as long as he had money to bet with, he was convinced his luck would turn in the end.

Dane, on the other hand, knew exactly how much Kelly owed him, and kept a running total in his head as the amount grew. But none of that showed on his tranquil face. For the first time, Dane was playing for personal stakes, and the outcome was too important for him to take any chances. His weariness was held at bay with an iron will, his concentration focused with all the mastery of twenty years of practice. And, most importantly, he used his ability to almost literally detach his mind from his body. The muscular twinges of protest from a body held still for too long never touched his mind and, so, never betrayed him.

The game went on. Hours passed.

Since it was dealer's choice and Kelly favored wild cards, at least half the time the matches tended to finish with high-ranking hands. And since they played draw poker rather than straight stud poker, no cards were left faceup, so neither could measure the possibilities of the other's hand.

One on one. Skill against skill.

Gradually, inexorably, the pots began to increase, and the bets became tens of thousands of dollars.

The clock on the mantel ticked away steadily.

"Jennifer."

She came out of a sound sleep, instantly awake and sitting up, blinking at the light on her nightstand and then turning her eyes to the window. "Dane!" She glanced at the clock on the nightstand, puzzled. "It's almost dawn. What—"

"Will you get dressed and come with me?" His voice was steady, like his eyes. "There's something I want you to see."

"Of course, but—"

"I'll wait at the front door," he said softly, and glided from the room like a shadow.

Bewildered, she hastily slid out of bed and dressed in jeans and a pullover top, wondering what was going on. Why had Dane come here like this, apparently slipping into the house through a window? She felt uneasy, and something was nagging at her, some elusive thing she couldn't grasp.

Dressed, she left her room and joined him by the front door. He gave her no opportunity to ask questions, but simply led the way out to his car. And she said nothing until they were a heading down the road toward Belle Retour.

"So you finally got fed up?" she murmured. And felt his swift glance.

"What do you mean?"

"The Ferrari is gone." Her hand absently smoothed the vinyl of the seat between them. "No bucket seats in this one."

He was silent.

"Dane, what's going on?"

"Just wait, all right?"

Jennifer said nothing else, her mind busy with speculation. Had that last game gone wrong, was that it? Something he wanted her to see. What? And why was he . . . different? He hadn't touched her at all, hadn't tried to reassure her in any way. And that was very unlike Dane.

But she remained silent, not even commenting when, after driving halfway down the dark lane to the house, he cut off the car's headlights and almost coasted the remaining distance. She said nothing when he stopped and got out, or when he came around to her side and she left the car as well.

She just looked up at him and waited.

"Trust me?" he asked.

"Yes." But she didn't say, *Of course I trust you—I love you.* She didn't say it. And she didn't know why.

"Wait here."

Jennifer didn't see him leave as much as feel it, abruptly conscious he was gone. She stood alone in the shifting shadows, hearing the soft whine of the breeze through the tall oak trees. Her mind was curiously blank, yet her body was tensed, uneasy in some way she didn't really understand. She sensed that she was braced for something, instinctively or intuitively certain there was a shock in store for her. But she waited for him, there in the dark.

When he returned to her side, a bare ten minutes later, he made no more sound than he had when he'd left her. He was simply there, a presence returned. He didn't tell her where he'd gone or what had happened, but simply stood looking down at her for a moment. She had the odd certainty that he could see her more clearly than she saw him, as if she could feel his eyes, like a cat's, in the darkness.

Quietly, he said, "I want you to listen to me carefully. In a minute, I'm going to take you into the house because there's something I want you to see. But you have to be absolutely silent. If you make a sound, then you'll never have the revenge you want against Kelly. Do you understand?"

"Yes. I understand."

Without another word, he took her hand and led her to the front of the house. Jennifer thought about the security guard, but something in his swift, certain movements told her there was no need to worry about the other man. So she followed him through the front door he opened and then closed silently behind them. She followed him into the foyer, remaining near the walls where the old floors would be less likely to betray them with a sound. The house was silent, but as they neared one of the parlors she could hear the murmur of male voices from inside.

The doors were standing partially open, and only a dim light shone from within, from the far side of the room near the windows. Where they stood was in darkness, but she moved obediently to his guiding touch, slipping around him until she could gaze into the parlor. And it didn't take his grip on her shoulder to hold Jennifer silent. In her shock, she couldn't make a sound.

Two men sat playing cards in a circle of light from a low-hanging lamp. Between them on the round table was a pile of money and a number of papers Jennifer couldn't see clearly from where she stood. The men's faces were expressionless, yet somehow tense, deadly serious. On Kelly's face, the lamplight caught the gleam of perspiration, the throb of a pulse at his temple. She could almost smell animal emotions, like the fear of some beast at bay, cornered and desperate.

And that other face . . .

The guiding hand on her shoulder drew her silently back away from the door, and she obeyed. Her body felt leaden with shock, yet she followed him with no sound back across the foyer and down another hallway, until at last he led her into the study, where it had all begun, and shut the door behind them.

"They won't be able to hear us in here," he said in a quiet but normal tone. Then he sent her a flickering smile as he rested a hip on the corner of the desk. "Unless that temper of yours explodes, that is."

Jennifer felt no anger. Not yet. Now, all she could feel was shock, astonishment, confusion. She stared at him, noting the watchful eyes that had seemed so different even in the brief time she had seen them, set in a strikingly handsome face she knew as well as her own.

"*Twins,*" she whispered.

He nodded, still watchful. "I could hardly deny that, could I? My name's Skye."

"Why didn't he tell me?" There was still confusion in her voice, and hurt.

"He couldn't." His face, so like Dane's except for the indefinable difference in the vivid eyes, was serious.

"Jennifer, for more than ten years, Dane and I have bet our lives on the certainty that no one knew we were twins. No one knew there were two of us. Dane's was the public role, the well-known face and personality of an international gambler, a man who might be many things, even a thief. Trusted by intelligence agents for his information; trusted by criminals who were almost sure he was one of them."

"And you?"

Skye smiled a little. "I was the one in the dark, the one without a public name—unless I needed to borrow Dane's."

"You switched places?"

"A game peculiar to twins." His smile faded, and he was suddenly intent, grave. "But a very serious game in our case, Jennifer. Because of what we are, we have the unique ability to literally be in two places at the same time. All the records were altered, our names changed; Dane Prescott doesn't officially have a brother, much less a twin."

Jennifer was trying to think clearly. "I don't understand. What *are* you? Both of you?"

He drew a deep breath and let it out slowly. "Put simply, we're federal agents. But it's more complex than that. The two of us took the concept of an agent and—divided it in half. Dane is the cover. His identity is so deep and so completely real that no one with any suspicions could ever prove he was an agent. Because he *isn't*, not really. I am. I have the training, the official credentials. I'm the one who carries a gun and a badge."

Jennifer could see, intellectually, how their uniqueness could have been an advantage. But a disadvantage as well. "Then each of you lives . . . half a life?"

Skye didn't take the question lightly, laugh it off. Instead, he continued to gaze at her seriously. "We didn't anticipate how it would really be for us in the beginning. That Dane's friends would know me only as him, even though they were my friends too. That Dane would, over the years, often hate the role we'd created for him. It became a trap for us, Jennifer. We set something in motion—and got caught in it."

"No going back?"

"We can't, not now. Oh, we could both just stop, turn our backs and build normal lives. But if we did that, we'd be saying that the past ten years were just a game. That we did it all for nothing. And that can't happen, Jennifer. Because if it did, it would destroy Dane."

She sat down slowly in a chair, staring at him. Beginning to understand, now, one of the things Dane had said to her. "Because of his integrity."

Skye nodded. "I thought you'd understand that." He sighed roughly. "It went against the grain for him, leading the life he has these past years. On the surface, such a meaningless life. It's only his belief that we *are* doing good that's let him make the sacrifices he has. He would never have become a professional gambler if it hadn't been for me. Oh, he had the skills, but he never thought of making that a life's profession until I suggested it. Until I went to him after my own training with a plan. I believed we could make a difference, and he believed it too."

"So he stepped into the light," she murmured. "And you stepped into the dark." Even their clothes, she realized, reflected each man. And that had been the first thing that had almost unconsciously alerted her:

Skye was dressed all in black, a color she'd never seen Dane wear.

Skye smiled suddenly, a smile as reckless as the brightness in his eyes. "That's the basic difference between Dane and me," he told her. "We're both part cat—but different parts. Dane likes the sun; I like hunting in the dark. This life suits me, Jennifer. And as long as he can believe it has meaning, Dane's life suits him too. You see, the irony is that while Dane has the instincts of a gambler, he has the heart of an honorable man. It's always been a struggle for him to reconcile the two."

"Then, when he met me . . ."

Skye laughed softly, "Yes, indeed. When he met you. Your own father was a gambler, and you were hardly likely to want to get involved with another one. But what could Dane tell you? That he wasn't a gambler? He is. In many ways, it isn't just a role anymore. After ten years as a professional, it can't be." He hesitated, then said seriously, "We've both protected that identity with half-truths and white lies for a decade. And he couldn't even tell you, because we made a promise to each other that we wouldn't, not while we were involved in a job. A promise both our lives have too often depended on. And Dane has never in his life broken a promise to anyone. It's been tearing him apart, Jennifer, not being able to explain to you."

Jennifer. And Dane called her Jenny. Another clue she had unconsciously been aware of. She was silent for a moment, gazing at nothing. "Why have you told me this?" she said finally in a low voice. "Why not Dane?"

"He doesn't know I'm telling you now. He would have

told you tomorrow when it's all over and Kelly's in custody. But he wouldn't have told you what's going on in that room right now, and I think you should know."

Jennifer stared at him. "I don't understand." But she thought that perhaps she did.

"You talked to Dane about honor, didn't you?"

"Yes."

Skye nodded. "It shook him up, you know. You were asking the questions he's been asking himself these last years, and he wasn't sure of the answers. But I am." He paused, then spoke slowly. "I don't know about all twins, but with Dane and me . . . well, each of us has always understood the other more than himself. It's like looking into a mirror, except that what you see isn't a reflection of yourself, but another being entirely. And maybe because the surface is identical, we always see beneath."

Jennifer nodded slowly. "It's hard for me to really understand, but I think I know what you mean."

"Good. Then believe me when I say that I know Dane better than he knows himself. He's a good man, Jennifer, a better man than I am. He's honorable in ways most men have forgotten even exist. He hates lies, half-truths, deceptions. By nature, he's very open, and very honest. And he never breaks a promise."

She nodded again, accepting it immediately. "That's what I thought, what I felt in him."

"He's keeping a promise right now," Skye said softly. "A promise to you."

Jennifer felt a sudden tightness in her throat. A promise to her . . . "Belle Retour?"

"Yes. Dane's doing his best to win it back for you. And because he's doing it for you, the stakes are very personal this time. He's never done this before, played for personal stakes. That was always the distinction he made between playing a role, and *becoming* the role. It was always business, never personal. This time, he's crossing that line."

She stared at Skye, emotions tangling inside her. "He wouldn't have told me?"

Skye shook his head. "No. If he wins, he'll find a way to transfer the deed back to you and your mother, tell you that officials found a legal loophole or something. If he loses, he'll pull every string he can find, call in every favor owed, until somebody invents a loophole that does the trick. But he won't take the credit for it. Now or ever."

"But why wouldn't he—" And then she stopped, realizing.

"You see it, don't you? Dane won't ever tell you it was his doing because he loves you. He wants you to be happy, and it doesn't matter what he might lose himself. He'd never use that promise of his as a way to bind you to him. You'll have your home back, but you won't owe Dane anything for it." Skye smiled a bit wryly. "He hates debts."

Jennifer sat staring down at her hands. She was only dimly aware of Skye moving, and looked up to find him sitting on a footstool at her knees and watching her gravely. How odd, she thought, to look at that face and know this wasn't Dane. And even more odd to realize that she would always know which of the identical men was Dane. Always. Just as she had instinctively known there was something different when this brother had appeared in her room tonight.

And she understood the differences between the brothers. Loving Dane, she discovered that she intuitively understood Skye as well with a knowledge that didn't require time. This man, of course, shared the natural physical strength that was Dane's, the innate charm and lazy grace. But where Dane was tranquil and controlled, Skye was restless and reckless. It was in his eyes, in the movements that were quicker than his brother's. She thought that Dane's mastery of poker had helped build his control, while Skye's "hunting in the dark" had earned him sharper reflexes.

Dane was the lion, graceful in the sun; Skye was the tiger prowling at night.

"Why did you tell me?" she asked Skye.

"So you'd understand what you need to," he told her quietly. "Dane loves you. He loves you so much that he's willing to break all his rules for you. Rules he's managed not to break even during ten years of playing the part of an unscrupulous man. If he has to cheat to win your home back for you, then he will. If he has to risk everything he has, then he will. That's what you have to understand about Dane, Jennifer. When it comes to the happiness of someone he loves, there are no limits."

She was silent for a moment, then said slowly, "He thinks I won't be able to accept a future with him, doesn't he?"

Skye nodded. "Because his life won't be an easy one to share. This masquerade of ours works. As long as it continues to work, we're too damned effective as agents to turn our backs and walk away. And that means our lives are complicated. Sometimes dangerous. But, to us, the risk has always been outweighed by the good of what we were able to accomplish."

"A risk I have to accept," she murmured.

"If you love him, yes. He is what he is, Jennifer, what these last years have made him. We both are." He paused, then said, "He'll lose a little bit of himself in that room tonight. Breaking the rules does that, especially to a man like Dane. But the loss is worth it to him, because he loves you."

Jennifer drew a shaky breath. "Aren't you afraid I'll say I love him out of gratitude, now that I know all this?"

"No." His response was instant, certain. "You'd never offer any man a false love, because you're as honest as Dane is."

After a moment, Skye rose and took her hand gently, pulling her to her feet. "Come on. I have to take you home. The game may go on for hours yet—and tomorrow's going to be very busy."

"What will happen?" she asked almost absently.

"Later in the morning, a roving squad of federal marshals is going to find that press out in the swamp. Garrett Kelly and his partner will be arrested on the charge of counterfeiting. He'll never connect Dane to the charges. The marshals will make it plain they received a tip weeks ago, and have been searching for the press."

"So his cover—and yours—will remain intact?"

"Yes."

"Where will you go from here?"

He looked down at her gravely. "I don't know. That depends on Dane. And on you."

Jennifer stared up at him for a long moment. "I want to go back to the parlor," she said. "I have to see what's going on in there."

Skye frowned. "Jennifer—"

"I have to know. Did you expect me just to tamely leave, not knowing?"

He hesitated, then swore softly.

"There's another door in that room," she told him. "It was open, and it leads to a service corridor. We can watch from there, and they won't see us."

After a moment, Skye said, "I want you to understand something. Dane doesn't like what he's doing in there. If it had been Dane playing against your father in the last poker game, you would never have lost your home. Dane wouldn't have accepted it as a stake. In twenty years of playing poker, he's never taken everything an opponent had. Even when he could have. Even when it was in his own best interest to do so." Flatly, Skye added, "Even when that opponent was a son of a bitch, and deserved it if anyone did."

"Another rule he's breaking?" she asked softly.

Skye's smile was crooked, but not quite Dane's, his charm a harder, rougher thing. "He loves you."

"And I love him," she said in a steady voice.

"All right," Skye said finally. "Then let's go watch a master at work."

The door to the service corridor was open far enough to give them a clear view of the table and both players, yet was far enough away and shadowed enough to prevent them from being seen. They reached it silently, and both almost immediately realized that the game was much nearer its conclusion than Skye had anticipated.

On the green table was a pile of money, and a neat

stack remained in front of Dane. Kelly's money formed a much smaller and quite untidy stack. Dane's cards were facedown, his hands relaxed on the table. Kelly clutched his with tight fingers that showed an occasional tremor.

Jennifer watched, fascinated by Dane's utter stillness, by the tranquility he wore like an impenetrable cloak. His eyes were serene and without force.

Kelly shoved the remainder of his cash into the pot, and Dane calmly matched it—and then raised the bet. Like a blind man, Kelly reached for a small pad of paper nearby, laying his cards down and beginning to scrawl something on the top sheet.

"Wait."

Looking at his opponent, Kelly blinked like a man in a feverish trance. "What?"

"Before you throw another casual promise on the table," Dane said pleasantly, "it's time to redeem these." He picked up a stack of the small papers at his elbow. "I'm calling in your markers. Now."

Kelly's eyes widened at the number of papers Dane held. "I—I can't right now. A few days, and my bank can—"

Dane shook his head slightly. "Afraid not. I took the precaution of checking with your bank today. You'll forgive me, I'm sure; a man in my profession doesn't take stupid chances. Your bank account is empty."

"I have other assets."

"None to speak of. And these markers say you're indebted to me for half a million."

Kelly paled. "That's impossible!"

"Total them if you like." Dane's voice was indifferent. "But that's what you'll get. I never make mistakes with numbers." He stacked the notes again and waited, his hands folded peacefully on the table.

After staring down at his stacked cards for a moment, Kelly said hoarsely, "I have this place. The plantation. It's worth two or three million easy."

"It's mortgaged," Dane said flatly. "You owe the bank half a million too."

"The market value—"

"Is depressed at the moment. You couldn't sell this place to a dumb billionaire with a fancy for ancestors."

Kelly's desperation was an almost tactile thing, like fog hanging in the room, gray and wet. "It's worth a million at the very least," he insisted. "Hell, you could hock the contents of this house for that much!"

Dane looked at him steadily for a long moment, then reached into the pocket of his jacket and drew out a piece of paper. "All right," he said slowly. "This is a cashier's check for half a million. You sign the plantation over to me for this check, and your markers."

Kelly barely hesitated. "I will."

"Then get the papers and wake up your butler and his wife. The transfer will be legally solid, or it's no deal. I want witnesses."

Almost lurching to his feet, Kelly went over to the mantel and yanked on the old bell rope that was still connected to the servants' quarters. He tugged at it twice more before Mathews entered the room, dressed in pajamas and a robe and looking half asleep and considerably startled.

"Sir?"

Kelly explained what he wanted in a quick, rough voice, and within fifteen minutes a packet of papers was safely in Dane's pocket. Mathews and his wife retired to their quarters, bewildered but aware that Belle Retour now had a new master.

With Dane's agreement, Kelly placed the check into the pot and drew out half a million in cash, making it easier for him to play out the hand; Dane still had a stack of money before him, and the betting wasn't over.

Shakily, Kelly matched the last raise, adding ten thousand. Dane raised ten thousand, and silently turned his top card faceup. Kelly's eyes jerked toward it: the ace of spades. Swallowing, Kelly raised another ten thousand. Dane raised as well, and turned up the next card: the king of spades.

Twice more, with both men raising, Dane turned his cards faceup. Before him lay a possible royal flush. He tapped the hole card lightly with his index finger, as he had before in this room, and Kelly's eyes were fixed on the lazy movement.

"You've pulled that trick before," Kelly said hoarsely.

"Yes," Dane agreed. "The question is: Is it a trick this time? Aces are wild. It could be an ace. It could be a ten. Or it could be a worthless card. You decide."

Silently, Kelly raised.

Dane matched his bet. And raised again.

Kelly went still suddenly, his eyes skittering from the money he had left to Dane's remaining stake. And he realized then that it was over, that he had fallen blindly into a trap he couldn't escape. He had a hundred thousand left to bet. Dane had twice that much. There was no way for Kelly to win.

"Stop while you've still got something left," Dane said softly.

Kelly's shoulders slumped, then straightened slowly.

And all three of those watching Kelly could almost see in his eyes the forced memory of that printing press hidden in the swamp. "I fold," he said heavily.

No sign of triumph crossed Dane's face, and his voice was as calm as ever. "Wise of you."

Nodding toward Dane's hole card, Kelly said, "I have to know."

"It doesn't make a difference. I would have kept raising, and you couldn't have won."

"I have to know."

After a moment, Dane flipped over the card. It was the ace of hearts: a royal flush. Quietly, he said, "A trick only works once."

Kelly's mouth twisted slightly. "I'll remember that." He sighed, then got to his feet. "All that cash is bulky. I'll go get something for you to put it in. And . . . and I'll be out of here within a week."

"Fine." Dane remained motionless for a few moments after Kelly left, then one hand lifted to the nape of his neck and his eyes closed briefly.

Jennifer felt herself being drawn back away from the door, and she allowed Skye to lead her quickly from the house. Outside, dawn was just breaking. They got into Skye's car, and the quiet engine hardly disturbed the silence.

Halfway back to her house, Jennifer said suddenly, "Did you think Dane was bluffing?"

"I've never been able to tell," Skye replied.

She looked at him wonderingly. "Not even you?"

"Not even me."

The car pulled into her driveway a few moments later, and Jennifer hesitated before getting out. "The security guard," she said absently. "Why wasn't he around tonight?"

Skye smiled faintly. "He likes to take a nap every night upstairs, while his boss is occupied with poker. Last night, there was a little something in his coffee to make sure he slept soundly."

"That's what you checked on when you left me outside?"

"Yes."

She nodded, then said more intently, "I want to tell Dane about meeting you. All right?"

"I was hoping you would." He laughed softly.

Jennifer smiled at him, then got out of the car and closed the door. She didn't wait to watch him leave, but went immediately into the house. But she didn't remain there long. Less than fifteen minutes later, she was in her car and heading toward Lake Charles.

Ten

It was almost ten o'clock when Dane opened the door of his suite at the hotel, and he had never felt so weary. After leaving Belle Retour, he had driven into Lake Charles and waited at the bank holding the mortgage on the plantation. He wanted it settled, wanted Jennifer to have her home back again. He had waited until the bank opened, drinking cardboard-flavored coffee from a convenience store and pacing beside his car.

His business with the bank had taken more time and interminable paperwork, but since he had taken the precaution earlier to transfer his own funds to this particular bank solidly to establish his credentials, there was less trouble than might have been expected.

Now, all he wanted was to take a hot shower and change, and then go to Jennifer. He wanted to wrap his arms around her and fall into a bed with her, and not get up for a week. Or two.

He hadn't gotten the chance to speak to Skye this

morning, but he knew his brother would be alerting the proper officials and coordinating the arrest of Garrett Kelly. From behind the scenes, of course; Skye would make certain Kelly never caught a glimpse of him.

"Good morning."

About to lay the packet of papers on a table near the door, Dane swung around in surprise. "Jenny!"

She was standing near the couch, watching him with grave eyes, so beautiful it almost stopped his heart. "I bribed a maid to get in here."

He moved toward her slowly, unable to take his eyes off her. She looked so delicate, yet so womanly in a simple silk dress clinging to every curve, that he found it easy to forget the grim night behind him—and other grim nights—when he was with her. His chest felt tight suddenly, and he knew he was afraid. Afraid of losing her. Afraid that the secrets and demands of his life would be more than she could accept.

Because he had to touch her, hold her, he wrapped his arms around her waist and lifted her off her feet, kissing her with a hunger that hadn't lessened. Her arms wreathed up around his neck as she returned the kisses fervently.

"God, I love you," he murmured.

Her eyes gleamed up at him when he lowered her reluctantly to her feet. "I love you too. And those answers you were worried about haven't changed a damn thing."

He went still, searching her face with a probing gaze.

"I had a visitor around dawn this morning," she told him softly, smiling a little. "It was a bit of a shock. There I was totally convinced there was no one in the world like you—and then your mirror image shows up."

Dane swore softly. "Jenny, I would have told you about Skye as soon as it was over—"

"I know. I understand why you couldn't."

"What did he tell you?" Dane asked warily, slightly surprised by her calm acceptance.

Her smile widened. "Several things he thought I should know. And he was right. He obviously loves you a lot. Can I guess that you're older?"

Dane smiled despite himself. "By ten minutes."

Jennifer nodded, unsurprised. "Most of what he said didn't really surprise me. I did tell you I already had all the answers I needed, you know. That was true. But I suppose I can hardly blame you for doubting me after the way I acted."

"Doubting you?"

"Isn't that what you were doing?" she asked gently. "Thinking that when I heard the truth about your life, I wouldn't love you anymore. That it would change me somehow."

Roughly, he said, "Jenny, there are dangers in my life."

"I know that. I've known it for days. Those promises in your eyes. Promises of happiness and excitement—and danger. You always keep the promises you make, and I'm looking forward to all of them."

"Are you sure, honey?" he asked huskily.

"*All* of them, Dane. Because what you promise most of all, is *life*. It's the reason I fell in love with you."

He bent his head and kissed her deeply. "I don't deserve you," he said as he lifted his head.

Jennifer fought to keep her voice light. "You probably angered the Fates. I'm half Italian, remember?"

That reminder made Dane recall the papers he was still holding, and he hesitated before saying, "There's one more thing I wanted to tell you."

"You don't have to. Skye didn't just visit me; he took me back to Belle Retour. We watched that last hand between you and Kelly." She was smiling again.

After a moment, Dane said, "I'm going to shoot him."

"Kelly?" she asked innocently.

"No, dammit. My interfering brother." Dane was obviously uncomfortable, and cleared his throat before continuing. "Jenny, the plantation belongs to you and your mother. It's been legally transferred."

"And you hate debts," she said mildly.

"You don't owe me anything," he insisted.

Ignoring that, she mused, "You've got at least a million dollars in that plantation. More than that, probably, since I'll bet you paid off the mortgage. I don't see how I'd ever be able to pay you back." She shook her head ruefully.

"Jenny—"

"This is dreadful," she told him in a solemn tone. "I can't have the both of us worrying about that debt. Maybe I could sell the place, and then—"

"Are you out of your mind?" he exploded. Then he realized she was smiling again.

"Just wanted you to put it in the proper perspective," she said gently.

He almost shook her, torn between relief and exasperation. "Dammit, Jenny."

"Well, there really is only one solution." She reached

behind her to take the packet of papers from his hand and tossed them on the couch, then slid her arms back up around his neck. "You keep Belle Retour. You won it fairly, after all."

"I didn't cheat," he admitted, wanting her to know that. "But I spent this whole morning—"

"And I'll live there with you," she interrupted calmly. "I'll be in my home again, and I won't owe you a million bucks for it. Simple. Even an international gambler should have a base of operations, and think how your stock will rise when people find out yours is a two-hundred-year-old Louisiana plantation. Besides, it fits you even better than a riverboat."

He stared at her for a moment, then blinked as if to clear away mental cobwebs. "You must have gotten it from your mother," he said reflectively. "I noticed she had it too."

"What?" she asked guilelessly.

"The ability to make the most insane things sound perfectly reasonable. Jenny, I *won't* take your plantation."

"Of course you will. But we'll argue about it later."

He eyed her warily. "We will?"

She smiled up at him. "You should get some sleep first, though. You must be exhausted."

His mouth curved. "Slightly. Jenny, will you marry me?"

"Yes."

He lifted her off her feet again, kissing her. "Who's hitching whose fate to a rogue star?" he murmured against her lips.

"We both are, I think. And isn't it nice that I'm wearing them again, just like the night we met?"

"Wearing what?"

"Garters." Held on a level with him, she peered solemnly into his vivid eyes. "You know, those sexy little devices used to hold up stockings? They came before some total moron invented pantyhose."

He cleared his throat, then said, "Lace garters?"

"Uh-huh. The same as before."

In a single strong movement, Dane shifted his hold on her so that he cradled her completely against his chest. Then he headed for the bedroom.

Breathlessly, Jennifer said, "I suppose you can always sleep later?"

"*Much* later," Dane said, and kicked the bedroom door shut behind them.

Epilogue

"I still can't believe it," Raven Long said, studying Skye intently. "I always thought Dane wore more than one hat—but I never suspected there were two of you."

"You weren't supposed to," Skye reminded her in amusement.

She sighed, then looked at her husband, who was sitting beside her on the couch in their hotel suite. "And if Dane hadn't bolted off on his honeymoon, we'd probably never have known." Parenthetically, she added, "I knew he'd get sidetracked by that blonde."

Josh smiled at her, his normally hard blue eyes softened, as always, when he looked at her. "By now, we should have learned to expect this sort of thing," he commented.

Raven smiled in agreement, then returned her gaze to Skye. "But you said that security man of Kelly's had some interesting information?"

Skye nodded. "Very interesting. It appears he had a

brief stint as a federal agent about the time he was leaving thumbprints on the lock of your apartment."

Raven stared at him for a long moment, and then said hollowly, "Don't tell me—"

Clearing his throat, Skye murmured. "Afraid so."

Thirty seconds later, Raven was on her feet and pacing violently. *"Hagen,"* she uttered in a voice that made the name a curse. "He's gone too far, Josh, this time he's really crossed the line! I'll kill him with my bare hands."

Her husband lit a cigarette, watching her calmly. "Don't waste energy getting mad, darling," he told her. "This time, we're going to get even."

Skye, watching them, felt a stab of pity for Hagen. He'd seen smiles before like the kind these two were wearing; he'd even worn a few himself . . . just before all hell broke loose.

Coming next month . . .

The Pearls of Sharah II:
RAINE'S STORY
by Fayrene Preston

A thrilling romance set in London, **RAINE'S STORY** is the second book in the fabulous trilogy in which a seven-foot rope of priceless antique pearls mysteriously passes from hand to hand, forever changing the lives of those who possess it.

Michael Carr, as mysterious as he is attractive, meets the enchanting Raine Bennett one foggy night near Hyde Park. Immediately, he is enraptured by her . . . and suspicious of her, for she is wearing the rope of famous pearls that has recently been reported stolen to Interpol, for which he works. Now Michael must struggle to resist his mad passion for Raine, even as he tries to clear her name. In the following excerpt Michael, still very much a stranger to Raine, has surprised her by intercepting her and whisking her off for a picnic lunch.

She tilted her head, and sunshine caught and tangled in the long, gently waving strands of her hair. "Who are you, Michael Carr?"

He paused in the act of unstrapping two plates from the hamper's lid. "You know who I am. You just said my name, and I told you last night that I'm in London on business." His blue eyes sharpened. "What's bothering you, Raine? I mean beside the obvious, that you're here against your will."

"I'm not here against my will. I'm perfectly capable of hiking back down the hill and calling a taxi."

He rested an arm on an upraised knee. "Then what's bothering you?"

The softness of his voice made warmth shiver through her. She waited a beat for the feeling to pass. "I want to know how you arranged this."

"Raine, you should know you can arrange anything if you want to badly enough."

"Then you must be very rich."

"Not particularly. I'm just very determined. We're having chili dogs. I hope you like them." He delved into the hamper and brought out an insulated container. "With freshly made New Mexico chili."

"Freshly made chili? From Fortnum and Mason's?"

"Very early this morning I made the acquaintance of that good establishment's chef. He whipped this up for us from my own recipe."

She thought of the delicate cakes, tea sandwiches, and biscuits that the chef usually made. "I can't even imagine . . . he must have been appalled."

"I paid him a great deal of money not to be appalled."

She smiled in spite of herself. "You're trying to impress me, aren't you?"

He took her question seriously, gazing fixedly at her in an unsettling way. "Yes. Is it working?"

"I'm not sure."

"What does impress you?"

She made up her mind suddenly. *You,* she thought. But she said, "You never told me who you are."

"It's simple, Raine. I'm someone who wants you very much."